D1487145

Felicity~
A Sparrow's Tale

Felicity~
A Sparrow's Tale

By

Loralee Evans

Copyright © 2014 Loralee Evans

All Rights Reserved.

No part of this book may be reproduced, scanned, or distributed in any form whatsoever without prior written permission of the author except in the case of brief passages embodied in critical reviews and articles.

ISBN 13: 978-0692306918
ISBN 10: 0692306919

Loralee Evans
www.loraleeevans.com

Library of Congress Control Number: 2014918090
Evans, Loralee; Duchesne, Utah

Cover Design by Jacqueline Fowers and Loralee Evans
Cover Design © 2014 Loralee Evans
Illustrations by Rachel Evans and Loralee Evans
Illustrations © 2014 Loralee Evans

Dedication

To Tyler, Rachel, Paul, and Nichole

For their encouragement and support in writing this story.

"Hope is the thing with feathers

that perches in the soul..."

-Emily Dickinson

Chapter 1

*F*elicity perched on a leafy branch of her tree reading a book. Her beak almost touched the page and her eyes hardly blinked.

She had reached the most exciting part of the story, with the little rabbit rushing through the garden looking for a way out before he got caught.

She already knew he would escape, but that he would lose his jacket and shoes doing it. This *was* the seventeenth time she had read the book, after all. She also knew the little rabbit and his cousin would get his clothes back in the next book. Which she'd read sixteen times.

Still, Felicity always got excited at this part and she was glad for the quiet. She found it so much easier to concentrate.

Felicity was a small young sparrow with brown striped wings, a dark brown head and a little fan of a tail. She didn't stand out much from her friends, the other sparrows, except that she always seemed to have her beak in a book.

She had a whole shelf of books in the hollow of the tree where she'd lived since she had hatched, an old woodpecker's nest that their neighbor Augustus, an ivory-billed woodpecker, had given to her parents.

He'd given them the books too, and had taught Felicity how to read.

Since she was a tiny chick, the tales of adventure and danger she found in Augustus's books had thrilled her. She adored the heroes and heroines who forged ahead in spite of all odds, and who always seemed to succeed no matter what.

Sometimes, Felicity even imagined going on an adventure, and of being courageous and selfless like her heroes.

But when she was honest with herself, she didn't think she could ever have an adventure of her own.

There were seeds and juicy bugs to eat, songs to chirp, and best of all, books to read.

Felicity eagerly flipped to the next page.

But no real life adventures.

Or so she thought.

"Hello?"

With her beak in her book, Felicity barely heard the voice calling out and didn't look up.

"Is anyone home?" the young male voice called again, closer this time. "Oh! Hello, miss!"

Realizing that the speaker addressed her, Felicity snapped her book shut and tucked it under a wing. She nudged the book with her beak, making sure it was out of sight, then lifted her head.

"Pardon-" she began before she saw her half-hidden visitor come around a cluster of leaves.

She gasped, fluttering in shock. "A featherless two-foot!" Her book loosened but she caught it at the last moment and hid it under her wing once more.

The tiny man smiled at her surprise, but not unkindly. One hand held a branch above his head for support.

"Sorry. What was that, miss?" he asked.

She hopped a little, blinked her eyes, and fixed her gaze upon the speaker. "You're a-"

She tilted her head and ruffled her feathers. "You're a featherless two-foot. But a- a tiny one. I've never seen one my size. The rest are all big and noisy. And- they smell bad! They-"

Felicity stiffened and clapped her beak shut, cringing at what she'd just said. Had she hurt his feelings? Sometimes words just spilled out of her beak before she could stop them.

"Oh." One of the tiny man's eyebrows lifted and he grinned. He didn't seem hurt. "You mean- a *person*?"

Felicity tipped her head at the funny word. It seemed vaguely familiar. Maybe she had read it in one of her books. *"Per-sun?"*

"Yeah. That's what we call the big-folk where I come from."

"Where *do* you come from?" she asked.

The little man pointed a thumb over his shoulder to the forest that grew up tall and thick across the road that ran beside her tree. "The Wildwood," he said.

Felicity's eyes widened and her beak fell open.

The *Wildwood*! Where no sparrows *ever* went. Or any of the wide black roads the featherless two-foots made for their big noisy carts. No wonder she'd never met anyone like him. She'd never been in the Wildwood. She hadn't even flown over the road that ran between her tree and the thick forest on the other side.

She turned her head and studied her new visitor, wondering what he could be.

Wind caught at the tiny man's sand-colored hair and fluttered it about his head and pointed ears.

Felicity tipped her head. Big featherless two-foots didn't have *pointed* ears!

Something behind him shimmered as he moved, and Felicity hopped backward, gaping at the translucent wings on his back. She hadn't noticed them before. Bright and sheer like a dragonfly's wings, they caught the light, reflecting a rainbow's hue of colors.

And the clothes he wore didn't look a thing like what the big featherless two-foots wore, or even the rabbits in her book. A pair of pants, a long belted shirt and boots that went about halfway to the tiny man's knees all looked like they'd been made of leaves, all sewn together.

"Gracious!" she said, blinking her widened eyes at him. "You're a-"

She had read about them in one of Augustus's books but she'd never imagined she'd ever meet one. "You're a *fairy*!"

"Yes miss, I am," the tiny man said. His wings lifted him off his branch and he drew nearer, hovering a short distance away from Felicity. "And I'm looking for Augustus Ivory-billed Woodpecker. Is he here?"

He looked past her toward the small opening that led into her nest as if he expected to see the woodpecker there.

"Oh." Felicity dropped her head. "Well, er- He doesn't live here. Anymore. He gave his nest to my parents and, um, I don't know-"

"Okay, well, are your parents nearby then?" The fairy's brow furrowed a little. "If I could, I'd like to ask them if-"

Something on her face must have made him stop.

"Um, they're not-" Felicity said, her voice breaking. "They're not here either. When I was a nestling-" She swallowed. "A hawk ate them."

The small man's wings stilled and he dropped to the branch beneath him. He grabbed a nearby twig.

"Oh." His face grew apologetic. "Gosh, I'm so sorry."

"It's alright." A ragged sigh escaped her. "You didn't know."

The fairy heaved a deep breath. "And what about Augustus?" he asked gently.

Felicity shrugged. "I haven't seen him for a long time. He took care of me after my parents-"

The lump returned, and Felicity swallowed it back. "But I haven't seen him since I got old enough to take care of myself. I don't know where he went and I don't know if, um, *when* he's coming back."

The fairy's bright wings sagged, and his face made Felicity regret her words.

"You mean- you don't know where he is? If he's even- *around* anymore?" the fairy asked.

"Er," Felicity fluttered and hopped sideways. "I don't know, exactly. I just- Well, I haven't seen him in so long."

She took a tentative hop nearer to the little man. "I'm sorry. Were you a friend of his?"

"I never met him," the fairy said. "But my father knew him. Long ago. Augustus is the only one who could help us, with- our problem, so I offered to find him." The fairy shook his head. "And now I'll have to go home and tell him that I failed."

"Tell- who?" she asked.

The fairy ran a hand through his hair. "The king."

"Er, you have a- *king*?" She tipped her head.

The fairy nodded. "Taron, King of the fairy folk of Wildwood."

"You don't have a president or prime minister or, um, mayor?"

The fairy smiled a little at this. "Nope. Just a king and-" But his smile faded and he looked sad again.

"Oh." Felicity didn't know what else to say. The poor fairy. He looked so disheartened. *Maybe* she could help? "Um, I'm-"

The fairy looked up.

Felicity clapped her beak shut.

What had she been about to say? She was just a plain sparrow, not an ivory-billed woodpecker. The fairy had already said that Augustus was the *only* one who could help.

"I'm sorry for, um-" Felicity stopped. She didn't even know what problem had brought this fairy to her tree in the first place. She cleared her throat. "For whatever the problem is."

"Thanks." The fairy heaved a sigh, then managed a weak smile. "Well, bye."

"Bye," she returned.

His wings became a whir, beating at the air to lift him off the branch. He turned away and maneuvered out of the branches. Felicity watched him as he fluttered toward the Wildwood.

What terrible thing had happened? What had made him so sad? He hadn't said. Not that it mattered, since she wasn't Augustus and had no idea where to find the woodpecker. Still, she wished she could help.

The tiny fairy grew smaller as he flew across the road and toward the thick trees where the Wildwood began.

Felicity shifted her book under her wing, and started to turn away.

But then something, an instinct maybe, made her turn back.

Her heart jumped in her throat at the terrible shadow that cast itself over the fairy and grew rapidly larger. She recognized that shadow too well! Her book dropped from beneath her wing.

"*Look out, fairy!*" she screeched, flapping to the edge of her branch.

At her warning shout, the fairy looked up.

His eyes widened and he lunged to the side seconds before the hawk hit.

The hawk's talons seemed to barely miss him, closing on empty air.

Ha!

Relief washed through her.

But then it vanished when the fairy started falling, his arms and legs flailing as he plummeted toward the wide black road.

Chapter 2

"Nooo!" Felicity screamed. She shot off the branch and dove toward the helpless fairy. He'd be smashed! Why didn't he fly?

As she drew closer, she could see the terrible reason and flapped toward him all the harder.

Reaching her talons out, she snatched the fairy's shoulders and spread her wings wide, catching the air, slowing his fall.

The fairy looked up, terror written on his face as he grabbed her ankles.

"Your wings, your wings!" she wailed, beating the air to rise up with his extra weight. She looked down at the ragged shreds of the fairy's beautiful dragonfly wings. "The hawk tore off your wings!"

"Don't mind that! Look out!" the fairy shouted.

Felicity looked up and into the huge white eyes of a featherless two-foot's cart.

"Ahhh!" she wailed, flailing to the side just as the speeding cart roared past, whipping her and the fairy in a cyclone of noise and air.

The world became a blur and Felicity felt the weight of the fairy almost fly out of her talons. She clenched her feet, determined not to let the helpless fairy drop. She *would not* let go!

The whirling air subsided at last and Felicity righted herself. But she had no time to catch her breath when the fairy shouted again. "He's coming back!"

Felicity looked up.

The dark outline of the hawk bore down on them once more, swelling rapidly as it dove toward them.

Her wings already aching from the strain, Felicity lunged aside. The hawk flashed by so close that she could feel the wind of its passing brush her feathers.

A scream of frustration escaped the hawk. Behind her and to her right it wheeled around, its wings beating the air as it came at them again.

Flapping frantically, she shot toward the safety of her tree, the helpless fairy dangling from her feet. Any moment she would feel the hawk's sharp talons closing around her or ripping the fairy out of her grip.

Leaves slapped at her as she plunged among the rustling branches. In her reckless speed one smacked right in her face, blinding her for a second.

As she shook the leaf off her face, several twigs cracked beneath her.

"Ow! Geez! *Ow!*" the fairy cried as more twigs slapped against his legs.

"Sorry!" she gasped, struggling to pull his weight and weave through the branches at the same time.

At last, she reached a wide branch a few hops away from her house and dropped the fairy safely down.

She landed on the branch beside him, gasping. Her book sat not far away, its cover neatly shut as if nothing had happened.

Felicity struggled to calm her breathing. She'd pick it up in a minute.

A hawk's scream cut through the branches overhead and Felicity looked up with a start. Through the branches of her tree she watched the hawk circle once above them. Then it turned and flew off out of sight.

Felicity barely had time to feel relief when something touched her wing. She chirped in alarm before she turned and looked into the fairy's face.

"Are you okay?" he asked. He let go of her wing and rubbed his shoulder. "That was very brave."

Felicity heaved a breath. "Sorry if I pinched you. And for those branches hitting your legs."

The fairy shook his head. "You saved me. Don't be sorry."

"But your poor wings!"

"Yeah." The fairy looked over his shoulder and fluttered the remnants of his wings. "This isn't good."

Felicity spread her wings and hopped sideways.

"Of course it's not good," she chirped. "It's terrible. Your wings got ripped *off*! And-"

She stiffened and clapped her beak shut. What a thoughtless thing to say! He could see that his wings were gone. She didn't need to point it out!

The fairy's feelings didn't seem hurt though. "They'll grow back in a couple of days." He bent and picked up her book, turning it over in his hands. "Sometimes less. And they don't even really hurt."

He fell silent, and his lips moved as he studied the title.

Felicity tipped her head. Could he read, too?

The fairy looked up. "Whose book is this?"

Her eyes went to the book. "Um-" She gulped. "Augustus's. I, uh, I like the pictures."

She looked away. Well, it wasn't a *complete* lie. She *did* like the pictures after all. But what if he thought she was weird for being able to read? No other birds she knew, except for Augustus, could.

The fairy heaved a broken breath. "Oh."

She hopped backward then gestured toward the round opening into the tree. "Hey, um, you can stay a while. Until your wings grow back, anyway."

The fairy's forehead wrinkled. "I should actually-"

"Come on." She hopped past him and through the round entry into her house.

A little nest made of sticks and mud sat in the middle of the round room. On one wall hung a framed painting of Augustus's parents that had been there for as long as Felicity could remember. At the back of the rounded chamber a bookshelf that Augustus had carved from the wall itself held Felicity's several other books. Between the painting and the shelf sat an old-fashioned ice-box. Another gift left by Augustus.

"Welcome!" she chirped, turning to the fairy who stooped through the entrance, her book still in his hands. He looked around, his eyebrows raised. "This use to be Augustus's house," she explained.

She nodded toward the painting of the two ivory-billed woodpeckers. "They're his parents. My folks never wanted to take it down. Me neither."

She hopped toward the ice-box and opened it. "You can put that book on the shelf. I'll find you something to eat and- ah ha!"

She pecked up a still-wriggling beetle. The very last one. She shut the door of the ice-box and turned.

"You cam hab dis ome!" she said past the wriggling beetle in her beak. "Da guts are da bebst!"

The fairy stooped to put the book back on the shelf. "Did you say- *guts*?" he asked. Then he turned.

At the sight of the wiggling beetle in her beak, the fairy's eyes widened and his face turned a strange shade of pale green.

"Oh boy. I, um-" The fairy looked away. "Actually, I can't stay. Luckily- er, I mean, honestly I can't."

"You cam't go eiber," Felicity argued. "You mibe as well habe a snack." She hopped toward the fairy, the beetle outstretched. But the fairy scrambled backward like he didn't even want the beetle. But that was silly. Beetles were delicious!

She paused and shook herself. Perhaps it was rude to eat in front of her guest but it was just as rude to talk with her mouth full. With a flicker of her head she crunched the beetle in her beak. Tasty!

"Sorry about that," she said, gulping it down. She gestured to the icebox. "I don't have any more bugs."

"It's okay." The fairy released a breath. He looked relieved about something. "I'm really not hungry."

"Okay. Well, anyway, I was saying, your wings haven't grown back yet. So you can't fly."

The fairy's shoulders lifted and fell in a helpless gesture. He shook his head. "I've got to start back. I *have* to tell the king. Even if it is bad news. He's waiting for me to come with or without Augustus. My father will be worried if I don't get back."

The fairy turned toward her door and ducked out.

"Um, how are you going to do that then?" she asked, following after him. "You can't-"

Felicity stopped. Where had he gone? She looked around at the empty branch. But he'd just *been* here.

At a movement below her feet, she glanced down.

Her beak gaped at the sight of the fairy climbing down the trunk, hands and feet finding wrinkles in the wood. On his back, the poor remnants of his torn wings shimmered.

"Hey!" Felicity fluttered down to the branch next to the climbing fairy. "What are you doing?"

"I'm going home," the fairy said.

"What? You mean you're going to use your feet? To walk? Um, on the ground? Into the Wildwood? All the way to- wherever you're going?"

The fairy kept climbing downward but raised his face to hers, an eyebrow lifting. "Well, yeah."

"Why?"

He heaved a deep breath. "I *have* to get back. My father needs to know. He's the-"

"That's crazy." She hopped down again to the next branch. "You'll get eaten. Or stomped on. Or squished. Or- or eaten."

Now both of the fairy's eyebrows lifted and he chuckled faintly. But he kept climbing down. "It's what I've got to do," he said. "I don't have any other way to get back."

He looked down, searching for another handhold. The remnants of his poor mangled wings still reflected bits of rainbow.

He kept climbing down and seemed determined to keep going.

Felicity looked skyward for signs of the hawk returning. A tiny fairy walking (along the *ground* of all things!) would be an easy target for a hawk. And so many other things could get him just as easily. Foxes and dogs and cats and those big noisy carts the featherless two-foots rode around in.

"Hey!" she called out. "Hey, um, fairy!"

She fluttered down to him again. "I, um-" She shifted her weight. "I could help you-"

The fairy paused, and looked up at her. "What?"

"I'm not Augustus, but-" She cleared her throat. "Well, I could carry you. Um, on my back this time. I could help you. Get home at least."

The fairy's eyebrows lifted. "You'd do that?"

"Sure," she said with a shrug. "I'd be happy to."

She slapped the air with her wings and drew herself up. "I know I'm not Augustus, but I can get you home at least."

The fairy's face brightened a little. "I appreciate that. Thanks." He stepped onto Felicity's branch.

"My name's Colin," he said. "Colin of the fairy folk of Wildwood."

He held out one hand in a gesture that Felicity didn't quite understand but she got the idea that he expected her to do the same thing, so she held out her wing.

Colin took the end of her wing and shook it a little.

"And my name is Felicity," she chirped. "Felicity Augustina Sparrow."

Chapter 3

Shadows closed over her head as Felicity entered the trees of the Wildwood. She flapped her wings with determination, hoping Colin wouldn't sense her nervousness.

"Are you okay?" her passenger asked.

Felicity sighed. He'd guessed anyway.

"Yeah. Mostly," she returned. "It's just that I've never been in the Wildwood before. I've never even crossed the *road* before! It's-"

She looked upward at the branches and leaves intertwined above her head.

"This is kind of spooky," she finished. "Not being able to see the sky. Not hearing any noise the featherless- er, I mean the- the *persons* make. And-" Her voice tightened. "It's getting darker."

"Don't worry, Felicity." His voice grew sympathetic. "We'll be to my home before sundown."

Felicity couldn't see him where he sat directly behind her head, but she wished she could.

"Are there any, um, things in here that- that I should, er, worry about? After sundown?" she asked.

"Not in *this* part of the forest."

"O-okay." Felicity fell silent, unable to think of anything else to say as they flew deeper into the trees.

He seemed to sense her nervousness, and his hand touched her head, ruffling the feathers.

The trees grew thicker now, and taller. Felicity had to tilt one way and then the other, weaving around the tall trunks. A permanent twilight filled the forest, fading off into gloom and shadows all around her.

No sign of featherless two-foots remained. But then, unexpectedly, a narrow trail appeared beneath her. It looked too flat and wide to be a path for furry, four-legged folks. But it looked too narrow to be a path for noisy carts. It must be a walking path for featherless two-foots, she decided as it twisted this way and that through the trees.

Before it angled off into the gloom a rusty sign on a metal rod beside the path, flashed beneath her.

"Hunting prohib-ibited," she read aloud. "Oh, I know that word. It means you're not supposed to-"

"*Felicity!*" The word escaped Colin in a choked gasp, and her heart jumped in fright. What was wrong? But then he laughed, "You could *read* that?"

Felicity flinched, realizing her mistake, then heaved a breath. Well, he'd asked. She might as well tell him the truth.

"Um, yeah," she said at last.

"And those books back at your house- Augustus's books. Do you-" He paused. "Can you *read*, Felicity?"

Felicity cringed again. "Uh huh," she mumbled.

Colin didn't say anything right away, and for a long time, she wasn't sure what he thought.

Finally he spoke. "That is so *cool!*"

He didn't sound like he thought she was weird. In fact, his voice sounded happier than it had before.

"But-" Her brow furrowed, "fairies can read, right?"

"Yeah, we learn from when we're fairlings," he said, his voice bright. "But *you're* a bird! And you can *read*! Felicity, that is *great*! That is better than great!"

Felicity blinked, unsure why her being able to read had made him so happy all of a sudden. Well, it didn't matter, really. She'd just done something that had helped cheer her new friend up. *That* was what mattered. A grin spread across her beak at the thought. "Thanks, Colin," she said.

A chuckle, warm as sunlight, left his lips at this. "You are *very* welcome, Felicity."

The gloom deepened as they went, the trees growing more gnarled and fat, their branches thicker and more tangled above her head.

Felicity wasn't sure how much time had passed, when she felt Colin's hand on her head again.

"Just around this last tree and to the right," he said.

His voice sounded bright and excited. And as they rounded a fat tree trunk, Felicity saw why.

Above her, soft lights glimmered almost like stars in the darkness among the branches of three tall, slender trees that formed a perfect triangle. Lined with tiny lamps, little meandering walkways linked the doors of fairy dwellings that perched among the three trees' intertwining branches.

The fairy houses glowed from the inside with a soft, welcoming light, and Felicity caught her breath at the sight.

But the most impressive dwelling of all hung in the very center, a large round structure, suspended among the branches like a paper lantern.

"Wow," she breathed as she flapped her wings and rose toward the lights.

She could hear music now and voices too.

Here and there, fairies with wings like Colin's, fluttered among the branches or strolled along the walkways.

Her eyes round with awe, Felicity alighted on one of the creamy, smooth-barked limbs of the tree that formed the nearest corner of the triangle.

Colin slid from her back and landed on the branch. He trotted down the length of the limb and vaulted over the gilded handrail of the nearest walkway into the light of the lamps.

"Hullo! Colin's back everybody," an excited female voice called.

A group of curious fairies, all talking at once, began to gather near Colin. Some darted along the walkways while others fluttered in from the branches.

The men dressed much like Colin and the women wore leafy dresses over shimmering leggings that reached their ankles, with little slippers on their feet. All the fairies had translucent wings on their backs that gleamed like rainbows in the light of the fairy lanterns.

"What happened to your poor wings, Colin?" one fairy lamented while another asked in an excited tone, "Did you find him? Did you bring back Augustus?"

"A hawk attacked me," Colin answered the first question as Felicity looked on, still outside the glow of the fairy lanterns. None of the other fairies had noticed her yet. "But I was saved by-"

"By Augustus?" another fairy cut in. "He's here then? He has to be! He's the only one who can help!"

Felicity stiffened at this comment.

Several other fairy voices rose up but she didn't pay attention to any of them. She dropped her head, studying the drab brown of her feathers. She wasn't an ivory-billed woodpecker.

She had helped Colin get home and that was as much adventure as an ordinary little sparrow could hope for. She heaved a sigh.

"I wasn't rescued by Augustus." Colin's tone made Felicity lift her head as his voice rose up above the hum of the other fairies. "I didn't even find him."

His friends went silent.

"I was saved by another bird. One just as good as Augustus."

"Just as good?" a few voices asked.

"With a few talents of her own."

Felicity fluttered in surprise as Colin, and then the other fairies, turned to look up at her.

Colin smiled and gestured for her to join him.

"Come meet my friends, Felicity," he urged.

A wave of shyness washed over Felicity and she felt her face grow warm. The soft light of the fairy lanterns didn't quite reach her here in the shadows, and she was glad.

Ducking her head, she hopped down the branch toward the group. She paused, then fluttered up and perched on the slender handrail of the small walkway.

The fairies drew back, making way for her.

With a small hop, Felicity dropped down on the polished walkway. She found herself in the middle of their group, and her eyes turned shyly down.

"But she's just a sparrow," one voice said.

"And she's an amazing one, too," Colin added firmly. "This, my friends, is Felicity Augustina Sparrow. She risked her own life to save mine."

A murmur of admiration rippled among the fairies.

Felicity looked up, seeing fairy faces around her, all looking at her with expressions of wonder and respect.

"And," Colin added more softly, "she can *read*."

The fairies stirred and whispered even more at this, their expressions brightening.

"We should take her to see your father then," one of the fairies suggested.

"Of course," Colin said, patting Felicity's wing.

He gestured with his head down the walkway.

"Come on, Felicity," he said.

"O-okay," she said.

Colin started down the walkway. And Felicity, wondering why everybody seemed to think she was so important all of a sudden, hopped after him, flanked by the other fairies.

Chapter 4

The crowd of fairies had grown steadily bigger as Felicity followed Colin along the walkway. Many of them walked along behind her and her new friend while others fluttered through the branches around them. The news that Colin had returned must have spread quickly.

The largest of the fairy houses, the one that hung in the middle of everything, seemed to grow bigger the closer she got. Bright light seeped out through the walls. Two fairy soldiers guarded the entrance, clutching spears tipped with sharp rosebush thorns.

It must be the palace where the king was waiting. It made sense that this would be the first place to come, but hadn't the fairies said they were going to go talk to Colin's dad?

"Um, Colin." She reached out and nudged him with a wing.

"Yes?" he asked, turning to her.

"I thought we were going to see your dad first."

Colin's eyebrows drew together and his smile faded a little. "That's exactly what we're going to do."

"Well, um-"

The walkway that had been level before began to slope up a little toward the entrance. As Felicity hopped near, the two fairy guards took a step forward.

She stopped at this, and fell back a little. The sharp, thorny spears they held looked a little scary.

"They're friends," Colin assured her, putting a hand on her wing. "They won't hurt you."

Felicity paused, her eyes still fixed on the spears the soldiers held. "Well," she said, still uncertain at the sight of such sharp things. "Okay. But this is the palace, right?"

"Yes, it is."

She flutter-hopped up to Colin's side. "Isn't this where the king lives?"

"It sure is. That's why-"

"Does your dad *work* here?" The feathers of her forehead ruffled in confusion.

At her question, Colin's face melted into an amused expression and he paused. He turned to Felicity with a grin of embarrassment twisting his lips. "Oh. I thought I'd told you- but I guess I didn't. I'm-"

"Welcome to our city, Mistress Sparrow." A new voice, deep and rich, rolled over her in tones of mingled authority and warmth.

Felicity hopped at the voice and turned to look at a fairy standing in the doorway of the palace. This man had silver flowing hair and a kind face that looked a lot like Colin's. Along with clothes like the other male fairies, he also wore a glimmering robe around his shoulders and on his head he wore a silvery crown that looked like vines and leaves all woven together. His wings reflected the light of the fairy lanterns in glimmering drops of rainbow colors as he started down the ramp toward them.

One hand extended in a gesture of welcome. The other rested against his chest in a sling looped around his neck.

This had to be the king Colin had spoken of. King Taron. But what had happened to his poor arm?

"Um, thanks," Felicity said, her voice small.

The king smiled, and the resemblance between him and Colin grew even stronger.

"This is the sparrow who risked her life to save you, my son?"

"Yes, Father," Colin said, dropping into a bow.

Felicity hopped backward and glanced around as all the other fairies nearby followed Colin's example and either bowed or curtsied at the king's approach.

As the king drew nearer, she cleared her throat and dropped her head in as good a bow as she could manage.

Colin had called him *father*! That would mean that Colin was a *prince*. Why hadn't he said so before?

King Taron's uninjured hand touched her bowed head. "Thank you for saving my son's life."

Felicity looked up as the king drew his hand back. His eyes were kind but they seemed sad, too.

Felicity opened her beak but she couldn't speak so she closed it again. She swallowed and finally managed to murmur, "You're sure welcome. Uh, sir."

She cringed at her last word. How was she supposed to address a fairy king, anyway?

"Please," the king said. "Rise."

"Okay." She lifted her head, fluttering her feathers.

The invitation seemed to apply to everybody else too, for all the fairies straightened up.

"My name's, um-"

"Felicity Augustina Sparrow," King Taron finished for her. "Your parents were friends of my friend, Augustus. And you are his friend as well. And for that alone, you would be welcome. But you are doubly welcome for saving Colin."

His eyes went from her to Colin and back. "Tell me. What happened that warranted his needing rescuing?"

"Um," she began but Colin cut in.

"She braved the talons of a hawk to save me. It tore off my wings and left me to fall. She snatched me out of the air before I was smashed."

The king's eyebrows drew together at this.

"And she outflew the beast when it came after us again," Colin added. "Even with my extra weight."

The king reached out, gripping his son's shoulder. His eyes gleamed as he focused his gaze on Felicity's face. "I cannot say how deeply I am in your debt, Mistress Sparrow. Were I to lose my son as well-"

The fairy king's voice choked a little. Colin's eyes grew a little wet too, and he reached up, clapping his own hand on his father's shoulder.

"I'm alright Father," he said.

Felicity looked from one to the other, mulling over what the king had said. Were he to lose his son *as well*? What else had he lost? A terrible feeling settled on her. Or *who* else?

"Come inside Mistress Sparrow." The king gestured toward the bright doorway. "We have much to talk about, you and I, and Prince Colin."

"Um, sure," Felicity agreed and followed the king's lead, hopping up the ramp toward the palace door.

The king moved a space ahead giving Felicity the chance to hop nearer to Colin and whisper, "*Why didn't you tell me you were a prince?*"

Colin looked at her with raised brows then gave a chuckle. "Sorry. In between wanting to find Augustus, worrying about my mother, and getting my wings torn off, I guess it didn't come up."

Felicity opened her beak to give a retort but then she shut it again. He hadn't deliberately *not* told her. After all, Colin had other things to worry about.

But then another thought struck her. "Er, what?" she chirped, surprised. "Your mom?"

One of the fairy guards beside the door shot her a stern look and Felicity stiffened, realizing that she'd spoken a little too loudly.

But Felicity did not need the guard to hush her in order to fall silent on her own as they stepped over the threshold and passed through the bright doorway.

Her head lifted and her beak dropped open as the interior of the palace opened to her view.

Soaring columns of twining vines wove through the walls of the palace, hanging with lamps that looked like flower buds, light gleaming through the closed petals.

Several other fairy guards, dressed like the ones at the door, stood around the room armed with rose-thorn spears. In the center of the room a pair of thrones that looked like they were made of white, polished wood sat at the top of a round dais reached by three steps.

The king climbed the steps now. As he turned and sank down into one throne, his smile faded a little and the sadness in his eyes deepened.

"Come, Mistress Sparrow," he said, gesturing with his uninjured hand for Felicity to come forward.

She paused, hesitant. But Colin gave her a gentle pat. "Go on, Felicity," he said. "I'm right here."

What could the king have to talk to her about? She wasn't Augustus. She was just a plain little sparrow that until today had never even crossed the featherless two-foots' road let alone gone into the Wildwood.

She took a hesitant hop, then another.

Felicity turned to meet Colin's gaze. He gave her a hopeful grin. She looked back at the king. His face seemed kind but also sad. Her gaze flitted to the empty throne beside the king's. What had happened to Colin's mom? Was *that* what the king brought her here to talk about? But what could *she* do?

She had so many questions, but she didn't dare to ask a single one. At least not right now. She might say something stupid, or rude.

She swallowed hard, determined to be as careful as she could about everything that came out of her beak.

She bobbed her head when she stopped at the foot of his throne.

"Hullo, um, sir," she said, still not quite sure about the right way to address the fairy king.

"Hello, Mistress Sparrow." King Taron's voice carried a note of humor above the sadness.

He seemed like such a nice man. She wished he wasn't so sad.

"I have a question for you," the king said and his voice echoed in the room.

Felicity gulped. What sorts of questions did fairy kings ask?

Big questions. That's what.

Felicity shifted her weight. Silence filled the room.

She turned and glanced at Colin. Her new friend gave her a faint smile and a nod.

Felicity turned back to the king. She swallowed before she spoke.

"Sure," she said. Her voice quavered only a little. "What was your question?"

Chapter 5

"Why did you do it?" the king asked.

Felicity blinked. "Um, pardon?"

The fairy king put his free hand upon the arm of his throne and leaned forward. "Why did you save my son?" he asked.

Felicity tipped her head. *Why*? Wouldn't that be obvious?

"I- I just- well-" She shrugged her wings. "He was going to get smashed against the road. Or squished by one of the featherless- I mean one of the *persons'* carts. And the hawk was going to eat him. And I-"

Felicity stopped, fearing that she may have rambled too much.

"I just *did* it," she murmured.

"Did you think *nothing* of yourself?" the king asked. "The hawk could have killed *you* too, young sparrow."

"I didn't think about the hawk," Felicity murmured. "I just didn't want Colin to get hurt."

"You have a kind heart," the king said. "And you did a very brave thing."

Felicity looked down, feeling her face growing warm. She shrugged her wings. "Thanks," she said to the floor.

"Thank *you*," the king returned.

She studied the pattern that veined through the polished white wood of the floor. "You're sure welcome, uh, sir," she said.

A long moment of silence passed and Felicity did not dare to look up. What should she do now? Was she supposed to leave? Was she supposed to say something witty or clever?

Felicity shifted her weight from one foot to the other, trying not to flutter or hop. That might be rude. But oh, it was hard to hold still!

"Mistress Sparrow."

At his voice in the quiet, Felicity gave an involuntary hop, her wings fluttering before she composed herself and folded them behind her again. "Yes? Er, yes, sir?"

"I understand you can read."

Felicity tipped her head. What was he asking that question for?

"Yes, sir," she said. "Um, Augustus taught me."

"Indeed?" The fairy king lapsed into silence. His hand brushed over his mouth and a distant look filled his eyes.

She turned and focused on Colin. The young fairy stood a few steps behind her. Seeing her eye on him, he offered her a faint grin of encouragement.

"There is something-" the king said at last, "I would like to ask of you."

Her focus jerked back to the king.

"Yesir?" she chirped.

His eyes grew sorrowful. "Were you to agree, we-*I*- would be forever in your debt."

The king fell silent again as he turned to the throne beside him. He reached out, running his hand along the arm of the empty throne.

A moment passed. Felicity shifted her weight.

At last the king heaved a heavy sigh and turned to her again. "My wife, Lilia, Queen of the fairy folk of Wildwood, has been kidnapped."

Felicity's beak fell open, a question almost spilling out before she clapped it shut again, her body tensing as she waited for him to speak his next words.

"By a wicked sorcerer."

Felicity felt her heart drop into her stomach.

"A- a- Did you say a- *sorcerer*?" she squeaked.

"Yes, he did," Colin said a pace behind her. "A very powerful one."

"*Um*," she choked. "You mean like a wizard? With magic?"

"Exactly," the king said.

"A featherless two-foot, with a long beard on his face and a big stick?"

The king's brow furrowed in confusion. He looked at his son. "A featherless-?"

"No, he's not a person," Colin offered. "His name is Grak the Night Hawk. He's a-"

"He's a nighthawk?" She swallowed at a thickening lump in her throat. "Augustus taught me about nighthawks. I thought they were not so bad. They eat only bugs and um-"

She let her words die away, fearing that she might be talking too much.

The king blinked his eyes and the sadness in them mingled with a flicker of anger.

"The Night *Hawk*, Grak," he said, "is nothing like other nighthawks. The true nighthawks, as you have yourself said, are peaceful folk and we have never been at odds with them.

"Grak, however, is a cruel, unhappy bird that lives alone in a cave high in the cliffs at the north end of the Wildwood. The only thing he has in common with real nighthawks is that he is most active at night. He came to the Wildwood long ago and claimed the north end as his. We fairies, and other good creatures avoid his domain as much as we can. He is a powerful enchanter and he hates all others but himself. Especially anyone he feels threatens his power. And he sees fairies as a threat to his power. The other dwellers of the Wildwood have taken to calling him a *Night Hawk* because he is seen at night. And only then. In truth no one knows exactly what kind of bird he is or where he came from, for he is slate grey and has no markings."

The king heaved a sigh and seemed to slouch in his throne as if he felt very tired. "He has not asked for a ransom or anything else. I do not know why he took her. Perhaps he saw my queen as a threat to his power. Perhaps he wanted to remind all the inhabitants of the Wildwood what a powerful sorcerer he is. Perhaps he was simply being a- a-"

Silence fell.

"A jerk?" Felicity offered in a timid voice.

The king hit his hand against his throne in frustration, and Felicity jumped a little. "Perhaps," he said through clenched teeth. "Only the goodnesses know."

King Taron looked up but he did not look at the sparrow. Instead, he turned his eyes away as if he gazed at something in the distance. "The queen and several other fairies were above the treetops gathering cottonwood down that day. The sun set but the twilight lingered and I suppose Lilia wanted to gather a few more tufts before coming home."

He heaved a deep sigh. "That is when Grak came upon them without warning. The others were able to escape, but he captured the queen and carried her away. We know where she is but we cannot rescue her. We have tried-"

The king's voice broke and his fingers touched the sling cradling his injured arm. "But Grak has enchanted his border so that fairies cannot pass it."

King Taron finished with a prolonged sigh and then a heavy silence filled the room.

"Golly," Felicity whispered. "I- I'm so sorry."

At her words, the king looked up again and a faint smile touched his lips. "You are a kind and brave young sparrow," he said. "And perhaps with your help, we can get her back."

"Pardon?" Felicity squeaked. She beat her feathers against the air and hopped backward in surprise. "You think that *I* can rescue somebody from an evil wizard?"

She looked from the king to the guards and behind her to Colin. If they had tried to rescue the queen and failed, what made them think that a mere *sparrow* could get past the Night Hawk sorcerer's enchantments?

"I- I'm not Augustus. I'm not an ivory-billed woodpecker. I'm just a sparrow. There are a million, a billion, a quadrillilion-"

Felicity stopped herself. There was probably no such word as *quadrillilion* and this was no time to be inventing words.

"There are many other sparrows just like me," she continued. "I'm not special."

At her words, King Taron leaned forward in his throne. He studied her, his gaze both stern and gentle.

"Oh, I must disagree with you, Mistress Sparrow." His voice sounded warm and kind as he spoke. "For no matter how many sparrows there are in the world, there is only one *you*."

She looked up at him.

"You *are* very special. Whether you know it or not."

"But Augustus," she said, her voice small. "He was the only one who could help."

"So we thought," Colin admitted stepping to her side. "Before we met you."

The king's fingers tightened on the arm of his throne. "After he took Lilia, Grak cast wicked enchantments and spells that keep fairies out when we try to pass his borders. But the enchantment that keeps us from crossing the border of his domain does not work on birds. A simple bird like an ivory-billed woodpecker or, in your case, a sparrow, can cross over the edge of Grak's borders."

"But- um, no other birds could help?" she wondered aloud. "I mean, well, the ones that aren't wicked, anyway?"

The king inclined his head at her question. "We have allies here in the Wildwood. Birds who are friendly to our kind and who would try to help save Queen Lilia if they could. But Grak knows this and has conjured up other spells, other enchantments that turn them back as well."

Felicity gulped. "What sorts of- enchantments?"

"Spells that they say- *frighten* them," the king said. He traded a somber look with his son. "Grak is clever and resourceful. One must never let his guard down if he is within the borders of Grak's domain."

"Oh golly," Felicity breathed.

The king heaved a sigh. "Despite these enchantments, several brave birds made it to the cliffside where Grak's lair is found. But there, they discovered one enchantment that none of them could get past. An enchantment that can only be undone with a certain password."

Felicity rocked from one foot to another. "But if *they* didn't know the password, how could Augustus know it? Or I?"

Deep lines formed on King Taron's brow.

"Because the birds who reached Grak's lair reported that just within the entrance there is a stone door shut tight that has as they said, *strange markings* scratched into it. Small, deliberate markings that follow one another in a straight line. Such were their words."

"Markings-" Felicity paused and held very still, mulling over the king's words. She tipped her head. "You mean- *writing?*"

"We think that upon this stone the password is written." King Taron said. His eyes held a pleading look. "We think that the one who reaches this door must read the words out loud and that doing so will open the doorway into Grak's lair. But none of our avian allies have learned to read. That skill, we thought, was possessed by no other birds but the ivory-billed woodpeckers. That is why we believed no other bird could help us but Augustus."

"Until we met you," Colin added.

"Yes." The king looked at his son. "To have even the faintest chance of getting inside Grak's lair, you must be a bird. And you must be able to *read*."

"Oooh."

Felicity felt a sudden weight in her stomach. Without Augustus then, she was the only bird in the whole world- well, the only one she knew of anyway, who could help these folks.

"A sparrow who can read can help just as easily as an ivory-billed woodpecker who can read," Colin said.

Felicity sighed a quick breath and fluttered her feathers. This was becoming more and more like the adventures in her books. Special missions, magic, evil wizards-

But *now,* it wasn't somebody else being asked to go save the day. It was *her*! Felicity Sparrow. Her own plain little self. She could get hurt. Maybe even eaten! After all, the fairies called Grak a Night *Hawk*. So whatever he was or used to be, he probably *was* a hawk or a falcon or something that liked to snack on small animals. Like sparrows.

Felicity shuddered. She very much did *not* want to face Grak the evil wizard Night *Hawk*.

Saving Colin hadn't been a choice. Well, *maybe* it had been, but it hadn't been one she'd thought about consciously. She'd just done it. But this-

She wanted to help, but she was *scared*! Was it this scary for the heroes in her books?

She looked up at King Taron.

Then she looked over at Colin.

The young fairy swallowed as their eyes met. It was *his* mom Grak had locked away somewhere, sad and alone and waiting for somebody, anybody to come and rescue her. The poor lady! Wherever Colin's mom was, she was probably pretty scared too.

At this thought, Felicity's tail fluttered and she lifted her head. If Augustus was here he'd say the same thing and she hoped he would be proud.

"Sure," she said. "I'll try my best."

Beside her, a breath escaped Colin as if he'd been holding it. Then she felt his hand on her wing.

"Thank you, Felicity," he said. His voice cracked as he spoke.

She looked at him, surprised to see his eyes shining with tears.

In front of them, his father rose from his throne and came down the steps. She could still see sadness in the king's eyes. But now, she could see warm gratitude, and hope as well.

King Taron strode toward Felicity, his wings glimmering in the light of the fairy lanterns. He stopped in front of her. His good hand reached out and rested on her other wing.

"Thank you Mistress Sparrow," he murmured.

Felicity bobbed her head. "You're very welcome, sir," she said.

And even though she felt a wave of uncertainty and fear as she thought about what she had just agreed to, Felicity still meant every word.

Chapter 6

*A*fter a lovely supper of sunflower seeds, oats, and corn (the fairies didn't seem to have a liking for insects, which Felicity thought unfortunate) a young fairy maid showed her to one of the spare rooms in the palace.

The warm nest of cattail fluff the fairies made for her was softer than anything she'd ever slept in and she snuggled down comfortably.

But once Felicity fell asleep, nothing but evil things filled her dreams the whole night. Spooky things that wooshed through the air, chasing her through a dark forest. Felicity couldn't see them. She didn't even know what they were, and no matter how fast she flew, they only got closer, and *closer*!

She woke kicking and flapping to see a shadow hovering over her.

"*Awgah*!" she squawked before she recognized Colin.

"Sorry," he whispered.

"It's okay," she said rubbing the sleepiness from one eye with the shoulder of her wing. It felt like early morning. A lamp glowed out in the corridor and shone through her open door, illuminating a small table where a breakfast of more seeds waited for her. "Just a bad dream."

"Are you alright?"

"I- I guess."

He reached out and gave her shoulder a sympathetic pat. "Well," he said, his voice apologetic, "It's-"

"It's time to go," she sighed. "Okay, then."

Ruffling her feathers, she hopped out of her nest.

As Felicity hopped through the palace a step behind Colin, she noticed that the torn remnants of his wings from the day before were gone.

Little wings, like tiny rainbow-colored flower petals, had sprouted in their place on his back.

Felicity smiled to see them.

Colin led her out of the palace and along the walkways of the fairy community.

She saw only a few fairies out now, flitting through the nearby branches or walking along the hanging pathways.

Even though she could not see the sky from here, Felicity guessed that the sun had not come up yet, and most of the fairies, just like her, were still waking up.

The pathway came at last to one of the smooth barked trees that formed one corner of the fairy city. Colin followed the path as it curved around the tree, and Felicity hopped along at his side.

The path ended at a small platform jutting out on the far side of the tree.

The dimness of the forest beyond contrasted with the fairy lights behind her, and Felicity had to blink as her eyes adjusted to the shadows.

King Taron, his injured arm resting in its sling, stood waiting for her as she rounded the curve of the tree. A group of four guards stood with him.

He smiled as Felicity and Colin appeared. And as she drew near, the king stepped forward and placed his free hand on her wing like he had the night before. His grip felt strong, but gentle too.

"Thank you again, brave sparrow," he said.

Felicity blinked her eyes. Words right now didn't matter so much. So she just nodded.

"I would like to give this to you," the king said, reaching into a pouch on his belt. "For my queen once you find her."

King Taron drew out a silver necklace with a white crystal dangling from the end of it.

Felicity bowed her head, and he slipped the chain over her neck.

The crystal disappeared beneath her feathers but she could still feel it against her skin.

"The lair of Grak is northward; that way," the king said, pointing through the gloom of the forest. "He should sleep as long as the sun is in the sky. If you fly quickly, you may be able to reach his lair, save the queen, and escape before the sun sets."

Colin stepped forward now, and spoke. "These guards have volunteered to go with you and guide you as far as they can."

He gestured to the pair of guards standing nearest to her. One had light hair, and the other had dark. Their hands tightened around their rose-thorn spears as they took a step forward.

"This is Giph," said Colin. The dark-haired fairy nodded to her. "And this is Kurk." The fairy with light hair dipped his head.

"Hi." She offered them a shy smile, comforted a little by the fact that she would have company. At least a little way. They seemed like nice enough guys. But she wished that Colin could come, too.

Drat that his poor wings were still growing back.

As if he sensed her thoughts, Colin stepped near and put a hand on her wing. It made her feel a little better.

"We will look out for you as long as we are able," the guard named Giph said.

Kurk added, "We're sorry we cannot remain with you the whole way."

Felicity straightened her posture. "That's okay. I'm sure I'll be alright once I'm, um-"

She couldn't say *on my own*. She didn't want to think about it. And now as she did, she froze a little.

What *was* she doing, going all alone into the enchanted realm of some wicked hawk wizard? A sorcerer who could probably turn her into a bug *and* chomp her in one bite!

Her heart stuttered and she thought about her home, her comfortable little nest and her books.

For a second, she wished- But *no*! She had promised!

Fluttering her wings and fanning her tail in determination, she launched herself into the air. Her guides lifted off with her, their wings becoming bright blurs.

"This way Mistress Sparrow," Giph said and fluttered off into the forest twilight with Kurk beside him.

Felicity wheeled in the air, glancing back one last time at Colin and his father, and the other soldiers.

Colin waved, and she offered him a fleeting smile before she turned and flapped after her guides, her heart throbbing with a mix of excitement and fear.

Without the sun overhead or familiar landmarks to help her, Felicity could only guess their direction as she and her two guides flew through the forest, around the fat trunks of trees and over or under fallen logs.

The two fairy guards, Giph and Kurk, seemed to know the forest well and she was glad they had come with her. She would never have been able to find her way this far on her own. Here and there, a beam of light made it through the trees, illuminating the forest floor and the fat, rough trunks of trees. But mostly the forest lay in a perpetual dusk.

She could not tell how long they flew through the forest shadows but Felicity guessed the sun was getting close to the middle of the sky when to her surprise, the trees in her path- *moved*.

A wall of branches and leaves grew up in front of her and the two fairies with a speed that astounded her.

The creak and groan of twisting, swelling wood and the whispering flutter of shifting leaves filled the air like quiet, sinister voices whose words she couldn't quite understand.

Felicity flapped rapidly to slow down then wheeled back to avoid the impenetrable wall of branches and leaves.

Behind her the two fairies pulled to a stop as well, and hovered in the air side by side.

"What is *that*?" she asked, alighting on a branch that jutted from one of the trees near her companions. Thankfully, *this* tree wasn't moving.

"We can go no further, Kurk and I," Giph said. "This is where Grak's enchantments begin."

"Only you can go past this point," Kurk said. "We wish we did not have to, but we must turn back."

"Once we leave, the branches will withdraw and you can go on," said Giph.

"Really?" Felicity shifted her weight from side to side. "Um, how- how will I know which way to go?"

"Come this way," Giph said. "We will show you."

Kurk and Giph rose up into the air, flying toward a narrow break where a thin spear of light pierced the thick canopy. Felicity followed them. She flapped through the gap in the branches and leaves, and emerged into the open air above the tree tops.

Felicity blinked in the brightness. The sun had almost reached the top of the sky, washing the green sea of fluttering leaves in warm light.

She fluttered to a stop and perched on a bare branch that jutted above the topmost leaves. The trees around her stretched to the horizon in an unbroken sea of green, except to the north where a long range of mountains, hazy in the distance, rose up into the sky. Her fairy guides hovered nearby.

"Up here, your sight is clearer," Kurk said. "You won't lose your way so easily as below."

"Still, the enchantment against us works above the trees as well," Giph said. "Look."

He pointed his rose-thorn spear several feet away where a lump of leaves and branches bulged and swelled like the hunched back of an angry bobcat. The leaves even rustled with a sound that reminded Felicity of a threatening hiss.

"Watch this," Giph said.

He gestured to his friend, and the two of them retreated a few inches. As they backed away, the swelling leaves began to ease down. But then as the fairies came back to Felicity's side, the bulge of leaves rose again, rustling, and whispering softly.

"Whether we try to fly into Grak's domain above or below, his enchantments keep us out," said Kurk.

"No matter where we try to enter, no matter how fast we fly, the wall of wood and leaves rises to meet us, batting at us if we get too closer," Giph said.

Felicity winced.

Kurk added, "And if we try to fly high enough to go over the reach of the branches, fierce eddies of wind catch us and fling us violently back."

"Many of us have been injured trying to get through to rescue the queen," Giph murmured.

"Ooh," Felicity breathed. She tilted her head and shifted her wings. "Is that how the king hurt his arm?"

"It is," Giph said, and Kurk nodded.

"But these trees won't-" Felicity shifted her weight. "They won't try to hurt *me*?"

"This enchantment keeps out fairy folk," Kurk said. "You are a bird and can pass where we cannot."

"Even so-" Giph cast a wary glance northward. "You must stay alert no matter where you are in Grak's domain. Be wary of *all* that you see. Let nothing distract you. And do not deviate from your goal."

"Fly toward that cliff," Kurk pointed his spear toward one peak that rose higher than the others, one side a sheer cliff of grey stone. "Where that ledge slopes down the cliffside, you will find Grak's lair."

"Take care of yourself," Giph said with a sympathetic grin as he and Kurk retreated a little way. "And may the goodnesses watch over you."

"Thanks," Felicity said. As her companions drew further away, the angry swell of leaves and branches eased down, and finally flattened completely.

Heaving a breath, she rose off the branch.

Swallowing back her uncertainty, she flew toward the same spot where just seconds before, the leaves had surged like the raised back of an angry animal.

But as she drew near, nothing happened.

She circled the spot and looked back.

The fairies each raised a hand in farewell. Then gripping their rose-thorn spears, they turned, dove through the small break in the canopy, and vanished.

With a heart that felt like a pebble in her chest, Felicity watched Giph and Kurk disappear. Then gulping hard, she turned and beat her wings in the opposite direction.

Chapter 7

*T*rees marched up the ragged sides and ridges of the mountains that rose in the blue distance. At the base of the cliff Kurk had pointed out, a pale green ridge sloped downward, melting into the ocean of trees beneath it. The cliff itself, a face of grey somber stone rose stark and bare like a talon clawing at the sky. It seemed like a dreary place where no one very nice would want to live.

It made sense though. In all the books Felicity had read, the evil guys usually didn't like living in cheerful places.

They always chose drab, inconvenient places like crumbling fortresses surrounded by lakes of lava or dark castles in the middle of ancient, over grown forests or dripping caves deep underground.

So it made perfect sense that a wicked sorcerer who happened to be a hawk would live on the side of such a desolate, forbidding cliff.

Besides the sound of her wings beating the air and the thump of her own heart, she couldn't hear anything else across the vast sea of green tree tops. No other birdsong or any of the rumbling that came from the noisy carts the featherless two-foots rode in.

Felicity had never been so far away from familiar things. She had never been this alone in her whole life.

And to make matters worse, she was in the realm of the wicked sorcerer Grak, the Night Hawk.

She shivered as she looked out across the sea of treetops that stretched to the horizon. This was very open, up here. Maybe she could duck down below the treetops, into the quiet shadows of the forest. It was shady there and she didn't have to worry about anything pouncing on her from out of the sky.

But if she lost sight of the mountains ahead, she'd lose her way. And who could say that she was safe anywhere in Grak's realm?

She didn't know what unpleasant things she might find down in the shadows and the dark, among the musty, ancient trees.

Her dream from the night before came back to her and Felicity wished that Colin was with her. Or somebody.

One thing was certain; she *wouldn't* turn back.

So on Felicity flew, skimming over the ocean of leaves. She kept her eyes fixed on the mountains ahead and the grey cliff where she'd find Grak's cave.

But something beneath her, just beyond the edges of her sight, caught her attention. She looked down.

Below her, a dark shape sped along against the leaves at the same pace she was moving, wings outspread like a bird. Felicity started in fright before she realized that it was her own shadow growing larger or dropping away as the tops of the trees rose and fell.

"Oh." Her voice came out in a breath of relief. "It's just you."

She beat her wings and the shadow beat its wings too. "I guess I have you for company."

She dipped her wings and glided to the left. So did her shadow. Then she dipped to the right. Her shadow moved with her.

Watching her shadow against the tree tops, Felicity only saw the face looking up at her through the leaves for a split second.

"Oh my!" Felicity chirped, flapping her wings upward in fright.

Woosh!

The face disappeared just as fast as she'd seen it. But Felicity felt sure she had seen something besides the leafy tops of the forest leaves.

She dipped her wings and circled back. She wheeled over the place where she had been sure she'd seen the face. But she couldn't see anything now. Maybe it had disappeared down into the leaves. Or maybe it had just been her imagination.

Turning again toward the mountains, Felicity pondered what she'd seen as she continued to fly. A pair of eyes. Angry eyes. And a frowning mouth lined with sharp teeth. Maybe it *had* been her imagination. After all, sometimes her imagination got away with her. And now that she was on a real life adventure with the threat of Grak the wizard on her mind, maybe her imagination was working harder than usual.

Felicity heaved a breath. Her mind *was* playing tricks on her. That had to be it. After all, she didn't know of any creature with such a face as-

Woosha!

Felicity shot straight up in the air. She *had* seen the face that time! The same wide, triangular face, the same angry eyes and sharp teeth! She *had* seen it, flat against the leaves of the trees, looking up at her!

Felicity circled and dropped back down toward the spot where she had seen the face. Right next to that bent twig that jutted up above the leaves. She'd seen it *right there*! But it had disappeared!

Was she going crazy? Or- had Grak just conjured an enchantment to scare her, trying to make her turn back?

Well, she wasn't going to let him scare her!

Giving a fierce chirp of determination, she shot ahead, her eyes fixed upon the range of mountains in front of her.

Shawoosha!

A flat triangle-shaped face shot up out of the tree tops directly into her path. Huge, sinister eyes glared into her own.

A sharp squawk escaped her and she banked hard to the left, barely avoiding a collision. Behind her, the face dove back down into the leaves as quickly as it had come.

On she flew, beating her wings harder than ever now, a new fear gripping her heart.

In the split second when the face had popped up in front of her, she'd noticed something dreadful. *It had no body*! It was just a head attached to- well, to *nothing*!

Ooh! Grak's enchantments were too much for her! He had *monsters* working for him. *Monsters*! Floating heads with wide mouths full of teeth that could open up and swallow a sparrow in one chomp!

For a few moments Felicity wished that she hadn't come. That she'd told the king she was sorry, that she couldn't help them and had gone home.

But as her throbbing heart grew calm, she pictured Colin's face. And then the king's.

And she remembered why she'd come in the first place.

Felicity released a shaky sigh. Remembering didn't make her any less scared but it did help make her a little bit braver than before.

Clenching her beak in determination, she continued on.

Shawoosha woosh!

Felicity shot upward, avoiding yet another flat, angry face that leaped into the air just in her path with, of course, nothing beneath it but air. And then she flashed past it.

Golly, how many were there?

And were there any more coming? That was the fourth face she'd seen. Or maybe-

A terrible thought came to her and her eyes widened.

Had she seen several different faces or the *same* creepy face?

After all, they had looked exactly the same.

Was there a single monster head down there right now, floating through the shadowy maze of trees and woven branches?

She shivered at the frightening image of a floating head bobbing along beneath her through the forest shadows, ready to pounce up right in her path and- and then-

And then, what? What did it *want*? What would it do to her if it caught her?

She couldn't say, but whatever it wanted, it couldn't be good.

Felicity struggled to think. What would *Augustus* do? Would he just ignore it? Probably not. It might not be smart to ignore something that, well, wanted to *eat* you. Would he try to outfly it? But no matter how fast she flew, the face seemed to be able to follow her wherever she went. And it somehow seemed to know right where she'd be. So trying to fly away would probably not work either.

Maybe she should try to confront it, from a safe distance of course, and see what it did.

Shawoosha woosha!

This time, when the face leaped out of the trees and into the sunlight, Felicity didn't scream or dodge it. She did something else.

"Hey! You!" she shouted, slowing and hovering in place. It strained her wings, but she could do it for a little while. "Hey, you- you *face!*"

The face did nothing.

It did not blink or smile or do anything. In fact, it did not even seem to have heard her. It just frowned and stared at her with glowering, unblinking eyes. Two little tufts on the top of its head, a pair of fluffy little feathers, twitched and quivered. But nothing else moved.

Shawoosha woosha! Woosha woosha!

To her left and to her right, two more faces flew up out of the trees.

Three monster faces surrounded her now!

Her instincts told her to turn around and fly away, to take the only escape she had. To leave Grak's domain and go back to safer places where crazy floating heads with giant teeth didn't jump out of trees and chase after her.

But she didn't.

She couldn't.

She wouldn't.

Because Felicity remembered why she'd come. And she had promised.

Instead, she turned to the face in the middle. "Hey, you!" she chirped, ignoring how tired her wings were getting. "I'm not going to say I'm not scared of you. 'Cause I am. But-"

The face folded in on itself, going completely flat, then unfolded again to glare at her once more, motionless and unblinking.

Felicity paused. "What did you-?"

She dropped down and landed upon a long leafy twig that jutted up through the thick leaves.

She fluttered her tired wings and folded them behind her, now more curious than afraid.

She puffed herself up, fanned her tail and asked, "What did you just do?"

The faces did not speak nor did their expressions change. Then once again the face in front of her folded on itself and unfolded again.

Felicity shifted her wings and tipped her head.

The face on her left folded then unfolded, just like the first.

Then the face on her right did the same.

And then she saw something she hadn't noticed before.

These faces *weren't* floating in the air. They were resting on skinny twigs that jutted up above the trees, just like the twig she perched on.

And those little tufts at the tops of their heads weren't feathers!

"Wait a minute-"

Felicity narrowed her eyes and hopped sideways along the length of her twig.

As she angled past the nearest face on her right, the body of a moth with two fuzzy antennae came into view.

"Wha-" Felicity muttered to herself. "You're a *moth*!"

As if suddenly aware that she could see it, the moth stiffened and turned away, showing her the backs of its wings again.

"I saw that!" Felicity exclaimed. "I was scared of a *bug*!"

She beat her wings against the air. "You're all bugs!"

What looked like faces were actually the wings of moths; the eyes, mouths, and sharp teeth were only markings on the wings.

"You're not scary anymore!" she said, narrowing her eyes.

She fluttered off the branch and toward the moths. "Now shoo, before I eat you!"

The moths seemed to understand this, because they fluttered up and darted away over the treetops, weaving and bobbing in their haste before they dropped down into the trees and disappeared.

Felicity sniffed to herself, then grinned.

For the enchanted minions of an evil wizard, the moths seemed pretty wimpy.

Hopping off the branch, she spread her wings and turned once more toward the craggy cliffs in the distance.

Chapter 8

*T*he cliff seemed to grow darker and more forbidding the closer she flew to it.

Even though Felicity felt pleased that she hadn't let the spooky-faced moths scare her into flying back to the fairies, she felt worried. What other frightening things would she find before she reached Grak's cliff?

She pondered this question as she flapped along, her shadow rising and falling against the tops of the trees beneath her, but now a little bit over to her right.

Abruptly, her shadow fell away and became a small spot of dark against waving tops of grass.

Felicity blinked at the unexpected disappearance of the trees as a wide clearing spread out below her, walled in all around by tall trees and carpeted with thick grass.

Felicity glanced from one edge of the clearing to the other. This treeless space seemed harmless enough for being in the middle of an evil wizard's domain. It didn't look very remarkable either, except for a long chain-link fence that stretched down the middle of the clearing. The fence didn't look like it had been put there recently. Rust caked the evenly spaced poles that held up the fence and discolored many of the woven wires that formed the diamond shaped links.

From what Felicity could see, the fence didn't stop at the edges of the clearing but continued on into the shadows of the forest. As if the fence went on indefinitely, almost like the impenetrable wall of a fortress or medieval city. A little stream even trickled across the clearing, parallel to the near side of the fence, like a castle's moat.

But unlike the high walls and towers that the magicians in her stories built around their own dreary keeps, the fence couldn't have been put here by Grak. Fences were only built by featherless two-foots, the creatures that the fairy folk called *persons* (a funny word Felicity thought, that didn't mean anything much). No hawk could go and build a chain-link fence. Even if he *was* the most powerful sorcerer in the world.

Felicity dropped from the air, slowing her flight as she neared the fence.

As she darted over the stream, her shadow tumbled down into the water, crossed the pebbly floor, and rose out on the other side, dancing over the waving tops of the grass.

Nearing the fence, she noticed a rusted sign wired to the diamond shaped rungs pronouncing the weather-faded order that there must be:

Ignoring the sign's edict, Felicity settled in a crook of one of the topmost links of the fence.

She folded her wings and looked down, inspecting the worn metal beneath her toes. She flutter hopped from one piece of twisted wire to the next, gripping it and testing it with her talons. It was a real fence, alright. Not a massive stone wall disguised as a fence. And aside from being where no featherless two-foots had been in a long time, it didn't seem to be much different from any other chain link fence she'd ever seen.

It didn't seem to possess any particular magical qualities. And despite the sign, it didn't seem very able to actually keep any trespassers out.

Still, with what she had seen already, it might be a good idea to try and keep an open mind. Felicity had learned from her encounter with the moths that she could not trust anything in Grak's domain to be what it appeared. Perhaps featherless two-foots had put this fence here long ago, but now, more than likely, Grak used it for his own devious plans.

Looking around, Felicity's eyes trailed to two parallel tracks that ran along the north side of the fence from one end of the clearing to the other.

"Wheel tracks!" she whispered to herself. "Made by featherless two-foots' carts!"

She fluttered her wings and fanned her tail, pleased that she recognized what they were. But the little road hadn't been traveled in a long time. The tall grass growing beside and between the wheel ruts made them almost invisible, except from here, where she perched atop the fence.

Felicity beat her wings and looked up. The sun had passed the middle of the sky, and was slowly sliding down toward the west. She should keep moving. Especially if something wicked lived around here that she hadn't seen yet. Best to get past it before it scared the wits out of her like the moths had. Fanning her tail, she bent her legs to launch off of the fence when something on the ground in one of the grassless wheel tracks caught her attention.

Felicity's eyes opened wide and then a smile spread across her beak at the sight of the fat beetle trundling along over the dirt. Oh, it looked juicy!

Diving off the fence, Felicity swooped down and landed on the ground beside the beetle.

"Hello!" she chirped before snatching the beetle up in her beak. Its six legs wiggled in the air as she prepared to munch it down.

"Well, hello yourssself, sssparrow," said a smooth voice.

Surprised, Felicity spat out the bug. She eyed it suspiciously as it rolled to its feet and continued creeping along on its way. It seemed hardly put out that it had almost been eaten.

"*You* didn't say anything," she muttered accusingly as the bug disappeared in the tall grass.

"Of courssse it didn't sssay anything," the same silky smooth voice replied. "Sssilly sssparrow. It'sss an insssect. Insssectsss don't ssspeak."

The voice had come from behind her.

Fluttering around, Felicity's eyes went wide at the sight of the strange creature that looked at her from the tall forest of grass.

Unblinking black eyes studied her from a long face covered in shining scales. Its head gleamed black, while its chin and throat were pale; almost white.

"Um, hello," she said.

"Greetingsss." A long tongue, forked and pointy at the end came from between its motionless lips, waved in the air a moment and then disappeared back into its mouth.

The face, nearly lying on the ground, moved forward out of the grass toward her. Its eyes sparkled, yet its expression stayed blank.

Good gracious. This had to be another enchantment of Grak's. There was nothing else it could be.

Felicity hopped backward, and backward again. She blinked her eyes and shook her head. She *had* to be seeing things. This creature, whoever it was, had *no* legs! Just a head and a long, *long* body. She couldn't even see the end of it yet. The creature just kept coming. And *coming*. It reminded her of- those thick wires that featherless two-foots strung between tall, leafless trees. Did it have any end to it?

Even though she could see nothing about it that seemed dangerous (how could it be, when it didn't even have any claws, or a sharp beak?) she sensed something ominous about it. Something that filled her with a vague nervousness she couldn't quite put a foot on.

"Sssweet little sssparrow," the creature hissed in a soft, sibilant voice. "What hasss brought you ssso far from home? Are you lossst?"

"You're- you're just an enchantment," she said to herself. "You're not real." She lifted her chin and fluffed up her feathers. "I'm not scared of you!"

The creature's expression didn't change but its eyes flashed as its long tongue shot out again from between its scaly lips, flitted in the air for a second then disappeared back into its mouth.

"Of coursse I'm not real," it soothed. "I don't exissst. I am jussst an illusssion. There'sss no need to be ssscared."

Felicity hopped backward along the hard dirt track, fluttering her wings.

Even though she couldn't figure out why she felt so jumpy, her instincts screamed for her to keep away from the creature.

"Why?" she asked, her voice barely over a whisper as she continued to hop backward keeping well away from the slinking creature. "If you're not real why do you want me to be *not* afraid of you? If you're not real then, well, Grak made you only to scare folks, right?"

The creature paused. Its eyes fixed upon Felicity. They didn't blink. *At all.*

Again, the long tongue flitted out, waved in the air, then disappeared back into its mouth.

"Sssuch a sssmart little sssparrow," it hissed sweetly. "Ssso many quessstionsss."

It crept forward but Felicity retreated several hops.

"Come clossser and I will ansssswer them for you."

Its expression didn't change but Felicity sensed an impatient tension in its otherwise smooth voice as it seethed, "Come clossser sssparrow. I promissse. You can trussst me. There'sss no need to be uneasssy."

"Hold on just a minute," she said.

If this long legless creature *was* just some enchantment that Grak had conjured, why didn't it want her to be scared? What purpose did it have if it wasn't to get folks to go away? Why did it want her to come closer if it was just an illusion, like the moths?

Well, no, the moths hadn't been *illusions* exactly. They'd really been there. She'd just misunderstood *what* she had seen.

Something inside her told her that whatever this creature was, it *was* real. And unlike the moths, it was more dangerous that it wanted her to think.

"*What* are you?" she demanded.

"Doesss the little sssparrow not know?" the creature asked. Its voice didn't sound soft and soothing but had grown harsh. Its body folded tightly, its eyes casting off menacing sparks. "Then I will ssshow you!"

Felicity's eyes went wide. Some instinct twisted her insides. *'Fly now!'* the feeling screamed. And she obeyed the silent cry by leaping up into the air a split second before the creature sprang at her.

A chirp of alarm escaped her beak as her outspread wings thrust skyward. Glancing down, she saw for the briefest moment, the creature's mouth open just under her curled toes. Several small but sharply pointed teeth gleamed in the sunlight, its mouth so wide she could see far down into the darkness of its long throat before its jaws snapped shut and it fell back.

The creature tumbled onto the ground, coiling like a rope and hissing up at her.

"I know what you are, now!" Felicity cried, clenching the top of the chain link fence with her talons.

Augustus had taught her about these creatures when she was a hatchling. But she'd never seen one before. *That's* why her instincts had told her to fly away! "You're a- I remember now. You're a *basilisk*!"

Wait- that wasn't right.

"No, you're not a basilisk, you're- You're a *snake*!" She narrowed her eyes. "You don't want to scare me away. You- you want-"

"You ssstupid sssparrow!" the snake seethed.

"I know what you want!" she chirped, fluttering from one bend of wire to another. Her tail fanned in fright. "You want *to eat me*! You're just like a- a *hawk*! A hawk without feathers or wings!"

The snake slithered toward the fence, parting the grass to one side and the other as it came. Felicity shivered. Could it slither up through the links of the fence? She didn't want to wait around and find out!

"Come down, sssparrow!" it hissed again.

"No!" Felicity cried out. Spreading her wings, she shot up into the air, well out of the reach of the snake.

Beating her wings hard, she flew away, hearing the snake's angry hisses fade behind her.

Once she reached the northern edge where the trees began again, she slowed and wheeled around, looking back over the wide grassy clearing.

"*Phew*," she breathed before she turned toward the cliff of grey stone, larger now and closer than before. She was almost there.

But what other enchantments and tricks did Grak have in store for her?

Felicity swallowed hard. She didn't want to think about it.

Chapter 9

*H*er shadow skimmed away beneath her, rising and falling over the tops of trees as she went. Only now, it was further to her right than before.

As the day got older, the sun would begin to sink even closer toward the horizon. And her shadow would go further and further away.

The fairies had said that Grak would be sleeping as long as the sun was in the sky. But when it set...

A shudder ran through her. She shouldn't think about that.

She looked up toward the mountain that loomed above her. High up on the rocky cliff face she could see a narrow ledge leading into what looked like a low shadowy cave.

A heavy weight of foreboding settled on her heart at the sight of the dark opening but despite this, Felicity beat her wings with renewed vigor. As she neared the cliff, an updraft caught her wings and lifted her skyward. Ragged crags fell past her as she rode the wind up the face of the cliff.

As the opening drew near, she tipped her wings and fluttered to a landing on the stony ledge.

There, the cave waited; a dark opening in the grey wall of the cliff. It reminded her of the open mouth and dark throat of the snake near the fence, and Felicity gulped hard.

Drawing in a deep breath, she took a determined hop toward the opening. Then she paused and turned, looking out across the tops of the trees. The Wildwood stretched to the horizon, an unbroken sea of green. Somewhere out there, far away, Colin and his dad were waiting, along with all the other fairies, for her to return safely with the queen. And even further away was the end of the Wildwood, the dark road the featherless two-foots made, her own cozy tree, her nest, and her books.

Felicity pulled her eyes away, and gazed into the dark cave. She fluttered her wings, fanned her tail feathers in determination, and hopped forward.

She paused at the entrance and tilted her head.

There, several hops into the tunnel, stood a flat stone wall that stopped her from going any further.

And on the face of the stone, just like King Taron had said, she saw words scratched right into the rock.

"Oooh." Felicity hopped into the cave. This must be the stone door that would open for her if she read the password. Gulping, she perused the words before she shifted her wings and chirped out loud:

IF you WISH TO ENTER, My NAME THEN you MUST SPEAK.
I'M IN THE DEEPEST CAVERN, I'M AT THE HIGHEST PEAK.
I'M VERY LARGE. I'M VERY SMALL. I'M FLAT, I'M SHARP, I'M ROUND.
IF you WISH TO FIND ME, JUST TAKE A LOOK AROUND.
IF you HAVEN'T GUESSED My NAME, ONE MORE THING you MUST KNOW:
AS I GROW OLD AND OLDER STILL, THE SMALLER THEN, I GROW.

Felicity hopped backward as the echo of her voice faded. She tipped her head.

Any moment now, the stone door would do what magical doors did in the books she read. Either it would slide out of the way, disappearing into the wall, or it would swing open.

But it didn't move. At all.

She fluttered her wings and tipped her head. She'd read the password exactly as she was supposed to. Hadn't she?

Or perhaps the enchanted wall hadn't heard.

Felicity sighed, flapped her wings, and read the words once more; this time in a louder voice.

Still nothing happened.

"I think you're broken," she said to the stone wall. "I read your poem. You should open now."

Still nothing.

Felicity narrowed her eyes. "Stupid door," she muttered. She hopped to the stone door and pecked it.

Aside from losing a miniscule flake of rock, the stone seemed undaunted.

"Hmm," Felicity huffed.

What should she do? She'd read the poem out loud and still the door would not open for her. Should she turn around and go back? But what would she tell the fairies? That she had failed? That she had come within just a few hops of rescuing their queen and couldn't?

No! She was *not* going back! She hadn't come this far to be turned back by a dumb door that wouldn't open. There had to be *some* way to get in. After all, this was probably the door Grak used to get in and out.

Felicity turned and looked out the round opening behind her. The sunlight fell at an angle. Daylight wouldn't last forever.

Turning back to the stone door, she tipped her head. There had to be something more. And perhaps that something might be right in front of her face like the markings on the moths' wings or the deceptively harmless look of the snake.

Felicity's eyes moved over the words etched into the stone. Reading the poem out loud didn't do anything. So the writing itself wasn't the password.

Felicity puffed herself up as a new thought entered her mind. Maybe the poem gave a *clue* to the actual password. Just in case Grak forgot it.

A smile touched her beak at this.

Long ago, Augustus had read her a story about a small featherless two-foot who had gone on an adventure with some friends to fight a dragon. The poor little fellow had found himself in a situation kind of like this one where he'd had to guess the answers to several-

Felicity chirped and gave a hopeful hop.

"Riddles!" she cried out loud. "You're a riddle!"

All she had to do was figure out the answer to the riddle then speak the *real* password!

She grew still, and her eyes widened.

So what *was* the real password?

Felicity tipped her head, studying the words of the poem again.

"*If you wish to enter, my name then you must speak,*" she muttered to herself. "So- I need to say the name of- someone."

She fluttered her wings. Grak must have written the message himself, so-

"*Grak?*" she offered, her voice quavering.

Nothing happened.

So the password wasn't Grak's name. It would have been too obvious anyway. Wicked or not, he probably wasn't a complete idiot.

Straightening her body up, Felicity read the poem over again to herself.

"*I'm in the deepest cavern, I'm at the highest peak,*" she murmured the second line beneath her breath.

Golly. Who could that be? If she hadn't already tried his name, she would have said *Grak* since being a sorcerer, he might be able to go where other birds couldn't go. Hawks and eagles could fly to pretty high peaks but what could also go deep down in caves, too? Bats perhaps, but they didn't fly up to high mountains.

She puzzled over the thought, perplexed as she moved on to the next two lines which only added to her confusion. "How could you be large and small at the same time?" she lamented. "Or flat, sharp, and round all at once? And-" Felicity turned in a circle- "I looked *all around* and I still can't answer the riddle. That does *not* make any sense."

She glanced to the round mouth of the entrance. Was the sun sinking more quickly than usual?

"Okay, okay, Felicity" she murmured. "Don't get flummoxed! It's not good for thinking."

Turning back to the stone she mulled over the bottom two lines which seemed to be one last hint about the name of whoever the poem described.

"*As I grow old and older still, the smaller then, I grow.*"

Felicity shook her head at this.

No creatures *shrank* as they got older. They all started out small and got bigger as time went on.

Felicity looked down at the rocky floor beneath her toes. She had a feeling that the answer should be obvious. That she ought to know it but that her mind couldn't *quite* grasp it.

She returned in her memory to the story Augustus had read to her and the last riddle the small featherless two-foot had solved by accident. The answer had been completely different than anything he might have guessed on his own.

Felicity narrowed her eyes and lifted her face again to the riddle. Perhaps she needed to think a different way. She was imagining *creatures* the poem could be talking about. Of living folks. But what if the answer wasn't a creature at all? What if it was a *thing*?

If it was a thing, that made sense. But how could it be different sizes and shapes all at the same time?

Felicity blinked and her eyes widened. What if the poem described more than one kind of this thing? That might explain why it could be different shapes at the same time and-

Felicity's breath caught as she grasped onto the fragments of a thought. She grew still, fearing that if she moved, the fragile idea might be lost in the same way the weak shreds of a spider's web could be blown away by the faintest breeze.

Her beak lifted and she studied the words of the riddle once more.

What thing, not creature but *thing*, was at the tops of the highest mountains *and* in the bottoms of the deepest caves? What was all sorts of sizes and shapes?

What thing got smaller as time went on, not bigger?

Felicity dropped her eyes to the rocky floor beneath her toes then looked around at the ragged grey walls and at last up at the poem carved into the doorway.

What could she see all around her? *Right now*?

A chirrup of laughter escaped her beak. Of course!

"You're talking about yourself!" She flapped her wings in triumph. "You're a *rock*!"

The echo of her voice had not even died away when the grating of stone grinding across stone filled the little cave. Felicity fluttered as the door scraped open on hinges she could not see, revealing a tunnel that led away into darkness.

She gulped hard. Ooh, if only Colin was with her. Or anyone to help her be brave.

As she stood on the threshold, her little heart throbbing, the door started to scrape over the floor again. But now it was closing!

Good gracious!

Felicity hopped across the threshold and into the long dim corridor.

Once inside, she turned and watched the sliver of daylight rapidly disappear. The stone door shut with a resounding thump and Felicity fluttered.

Only a thin ray of light made it in through some tiny crack high at the top of the door.

Felicity turned and gazed into the shadows.

"Oh dear," she said and her voice echoed away into the fading darkness of the tunnel.

Chapter 10

*F*elicity hopped along the tunnel, listening to the beating of her heart. The little bit of light that squeezed in at the mouth of the tunnel had faded behind her. But as she continued deeper into the darkness and her eyes adjusted, a dim bluish glow began to illuminate the walls.

From its light she could just make out the rough contours of the cavern walls. In the darkness, the curving stone walls of the tunnel seemed like the throat of a giant monster. Felicity shivered.

The tunnel continued straight for several dozen hops before veering off to the left. The source of the dim light seemed to come from that direction.

Felicity drew in a breath, ruffled her wings, and continued in slow but steady hops toward the bend. Her throat grew dry as she went. She swallowed several times but it didn't help much.

She lifted her eyes to the walls around her as she hopped along, cringing at a damp streak that oozed down the wall. Her feet hit a slippery patch but she fluttered her feathers to keep her balance and did not fall. This did nothing to rid her of the unpleasant idea she'd conjured up that she'd been swallowed. Neither did the complete silence that filled the tunnel.

Aside from her own breathing, and the soft sound of her feet on the stone floor, Felicity could hear nothing.

Rounding the bend in the tunnel didn't show her anything but another bend several more hops away, this time curving off to the right.

How long did this tunnel go?

The faint blue light grew a little stronger as she hopped to the next bend.

Felicity's stomach twisted in knots. Pulling all her courage in, Felicity peered around the corner.

This new length of tunnel went straight forward for about a dozen hops then widened into an open space where the blue glow was strongest.

Hopping as quietly as she could, she moved along the tunnel and stopped on the threshold.

Her beak gaped as Felicity took in the large cave that opened before her. A floor of smooth stone stretched across to rocky walls that rose so high, the weak blue light almost couldn't reach the domed ceiling.

The light came from across the room where a ragged crack veined down the rocky wall from ceiling to floor. Where the wall met the floor, the break widened, making a small broken pocket of darkness in the base of the cracked wall. Up and down the ragged line of broken stone, something that looked moldy and dark grew out of the fissure, feeding off of the wetness that oozed out and bled darkly down the wall. And out of this damp gunk, a half dozen fat mushroom heads swelled, their plump bodies issuing a faint bluish glow.

The bioluminescence of the mushrooms glowed weak and pale. But as Felicity slowly turned her head, she realized that it still lit the room well enough to illuminate a hulking figure near the other wall.

In the gloomy light of the mushrooms, the sleeping creature looked morbidly headless, perched on a low rock that jutted a couple of inches from the floor. Felicity shuddered.

Behind the huge bird, a single mushroom grew within a little alcove indented into the wall. This mushroom glowed as well, exuding a sickly green light.

The effect of the green light washing one half of Grak while dismal blue light bathed the other half, added to Felicity's fear and she found herself unable to move as dread froze the blood in her veins. Grak looked at least ten times bigger than she did, even without his head. The little alcove in the stone that held the glowing green mushroom rose high above Felicity's head. But it barely reached Grak's shoulder. He looked so big that if he spread out his wings, they would probably stretch clear across the cavern!

Forcing her eyes away from the terrifying bird she scanned the cave, wondering where the queen was.

She shifted her weight a little, and the faintest glimmer of- *something*- caught her eye. She turned her focus back to the mushroom covered wall to see a tiny metallic gleam in the shadows where the crack in the wall widened at the floor.

She narrowed her eyes and peered into the deep, shadowy space.

Hmm. Something *was* wedged back in there, almost out of sight, and as she studied it, the shape grew clearer.

Tiny wires, bent and dented, rose up from a round base, coming together in a dome. A little arching door sat at the base with a rusty hook latched through a twisted loop of metal, locking the door in place.

Felicity's forehead wrinkled in distaste as she recognized what was shoved back there in the wide, shadowy crack. And she hated the sight of it, as any proper bird would. A *birdcage*! A birdcage had been crammed into that miserable little space!

And inside the shadows of the cage- Oh, it was hard to see!

Felicity turned and looked across the room at the sleeping hawk. A drowsy snort from the huge bird made her jerk and flutter back. But Grak merely shifted his weight and continued sleeping, his body swelling and shrinking with each breath.

Good gracious. She did *not* want to cross the room with that *hawk* there, breathing in and out and looking for all the world like he had no head at all!

But then she looked back at the cage in the shadows again. Was that the queen inside? How long had she been here? Colin and his dad had not said. And Felicity hadn't asked. Days? Weeks? Whatever it had been, the fairy queen had been in that birdcage way too long. Even if it had only been five minutes!

Puffing herself up, Felicity took a determined hop out of the passageway and into the large chamber. She looked over at the sleeping bird. Grak's body swelled and shrank with his breathing.

Felicity turned her gaze back to the birdcage. She took another hop toward the cracked wall, then another. Drawing in a deep breath, she began to hop more quickly. She didn't dare look over at the huge bird again or slow down for fear that she would lose heart. On she hopped toward the ragged opening.

As she got closer, the occupant of the birdcage grew clearer and hope jumped in Felicity's heart.

A figure in a begrimed silver dress sat dejectedly upon a stone inside her prison of tarnished metal wires, long pale hair hiding her face.

Queen Lilia! Felicity had found her!

The little sparrow reached the mouth of the small tunnel, and hopped into the shadow.

Either the fairy queen didn't hear Felicity or she didn't care, but the fairy didn't look up when the little sparrow stopped at the bars and peered in at her.

"Um, hi," Felicity whispered.

The fairy's head finally jerked up at the young sparrow's voice. Bright eyes gazed at Felicity in uncertainty. Despite the pale, gaunt look on the lady's face, Felicity could see the resemblance between Queen Lilia and Colin. Felicity's beak drew up in a faint smile at this.

"A sparrow?" the fairy asked, rising shakily to her feet. "How- did you-?"

"Yes, um- hello. My name's Felicity," she whispered. "I'm here to rescue you."

The queen tipped her head, the dull wistfulness fading a little from her face. Hesitant, she stepped toward the bars of the cage and grasped onto them. The fairy's long, silver hair hung over one shoulder. It would have been pretty except for the dirt and grime streaked through it.

"Where is Taron?" she breathed. "Why didn't he come himself?" Her eyes filled with fear, and her voice grew tight. "Is he hurt? Is he-"

"Heck no!" Felicity blurted. "He's- um-" She paused, remembering the king's injured arm.

She swallowed. "He's okay."

It wasn't *completely* true, but he wasn't *dead*. That was probably what the queen wanted to know.

"And my son?"

"Colin's fine too," Felicity said, looking away as she remembered her friend's poor wings. "They're both- they're both alright. But Grak enchanted the trees at the border, and fairies can't get past them. That's why they sent me. They needed a bird who could read the riddle. And, oh, they wanted me to give you this."

Felicity bowed down and the crystal necklace appeared out of her feathers. She bent her head and caught the crystal in her beak.

Speaking past the gem she said, "King Taron gabe me dis for you."

The queen's eyes became shiny with tears, even as she laughed a little. One hand lifted to cover her mouth. "May I have it?" she said, her voice quavering.

"Surbe," Felicity mumbled, stepping to the bars. "Id's yourbs, anybay."

The queen reached a hand through the narrow space. Felicity released the crystal into the queen's hand then bowed so that the chain could slide over her neck and off her head.

Queen Lilia pulled the necklace into the cage and held it close to her heart with both hands. The fairy seemed to be crying a little. But she managed to look up and give Felicity a brave but trembling smile.

"Thank you, brave sparrow. Thank you so much," the queen said, her voice quivering.

"You're welcome, um, ma'am," Felicity said, realizing that she had no more idea how to address the queen of the fairies than she had the king. She shifted her wings. "Now, all I have to do is get you out."

The queen heaved a sigh and her smile faded. "Escaping is not as easy as you might think."

"That's alright," Felicity returned.

She hopped to the door where the rusty hook held it in place through the loop. It looked loose. It even jiggled a little when Felicity nudged the door.

"It's just a rusty little hook." She bent and took the hook in her beak. "I'll hab you out ibm two-"

Though the hook seemed loose where it stuck through the loop of the door, it didn't budge when she tried to pull it free.

Felicity let go and stepped back, studying the hook. It didn't look very tight.

"Come on," she muttered before she seized it again in her beak and gave a more forceful tug.

It did not move.

"It's no use," the queen explained. "It's locked in place with magic."

Felicity's heart sank at these words while she spat out the taste of rusty metal.

She took an experimental peck at one of the tarnished bars. Despite being thin, the wire was strong and unbending. Augustus would have been strong enough to bend the wires back, she lamented silently.

Out loud she said, "There's got to be a way to get you out."

"There may be," Queen Lilia said. "But I'm afraid it will be rather- difficult."

The queen sighed, then pointed over at Grak. "Do you see that pattern of stones?"

Felicity turned and looked up at the gigantic sleeping bird bathed in eerie mushroom light.

"There. On the wall of the little hollow behind Grak," the queen said. "Just above the green mushroom."

Felicity saw it now. She had not noticed before, but on the back wall of the alcove where the green mushroom grew, a little square of nine small stones reflected the mushroom's green light. Three small rows set one above the other.

"Oh. Yes," she said.

"Sometimes, Grak has me clean his cave. When he lets me out, he pecks a pattern in those stones, and the door opens."

"Those stones?" Felicity said with a shudder. "That's the only way to let you out?"

With sad eyes the queen looked down at the crystal necklace she held in both hands. "I'm afraid so."

Chapter 11

Determined to stay hopeful, Felicity shifted her weight and fluttered her wings. "And which stones did Grak push?"

Queen Lilia heaved a sigh.

"I only wish I knew," she said. "He's very careful to hide which stones he pecks. I've only seen him press the upper right one once. Then his back blocked the rest."

Felicity's head sagged.

If she possessed magical powers like the heroes in some of her books, she could wave her wand and open the queen's cell. But she had neither wand nor magic. She didn't even have a good pecking beak or strong talons like Augustus.

"But that would mean I would have to go over there, right there where Grak is, and fly up to that shelf," Felicity whispered. "I have to go right *past* him!"

Queen Lilia's hands tightened around the bars of her cage.

"It *is* terribly dangerous for you," she said, her voice softening with sympathy. "Grak doesn't seem to want to hurt me, other than keeping me prisoner. But he would *eat* you if he caught you. I would not blame you if-"

"But he'll keep you locked up the rest of your life if I don't get you out," Felicity said. "That's about as bad."

Felicity lifted her head, and saw the kindness and sympathy in the queen's gaze. She remembered Colin's face, and the king's. She could not let them down.

"I'm *going* to get you out!"

Queen Lilia reached through the bars of her prison and touched Felicity on the wing. Just like the king had, and Colin. Her eyes delved into Felicity's. "Be careful."

Felicity smiled a little. "Okay."

Turning toward the giant bird, the little sparrow drew in a deep breath.

And despite the dread that made her legs feel heavy and her stomach clench, she hopped out onto the floor of the cave.

She took a hop toward Grak.

Then another one.

Felicity's throat grew drier the closer she hopped toward the enormous sleeping bird. But she did not let herself stop.

Grak seemed to swell in size as she drew nearer. And as she hopped closer, a smell began to waft through the air.

It was a harsh, wild smell.

And it scared her.

In spite of her fear, Felicity forced her feet to keep hopping.

The huge bird did not move except for the steady rise and fall of his breath. But this did not help her feel any better.

At last she found herself at his feet staring up at his seemingly headless body. A giant monolith washed in pale blue light on one side and weak green light on the other.

A single molted feather, dirty grey, lay on the stone floor at his feet.

Felicity gaped at its size.

Just one of his feathers was longer than her whole body!

And more frightening than the size of his feather, Grak's talons looked large enough to curl clear around her. *Twice!* The hawk's sharp claws glimmered wickedly in the pale light of the mushrooms where they gripped the stone perch that stuck up from the floor.

The huge bird's harsh scent filled her nostrils, stiffening Felicity's limbs into bits of wood.

"*Felicity Sparrow!*" the fairy queen hissed behind her. "*Don't let him frighten you!*"

Too late for that, Felicity thought.

Still, the queen's words helped Felicity gain enough strength to pull herself out of her stupor and tear her eyes from the towering bird.

Shaking her head to clear her thinking, Felicity hopped around him to the stone wall that rose up in front of her face.

Above her, the light from the green mushroom glowed out from the shallow alcove in the wall.

Hopping into the air, she fluttered up until her feet caught on a pebble jutting out from the lip of the little hollow.

Grak was right behind her now. She could hear his deep, steady breathing and she felt tempted to turn and look.

But she didn't.

Instead, she focused her eyes on the contents of the little alcove.

The glowing mushroom grew up out of a bed of moist- *gunk* and illuminated the rows of stones on the wall behind it.

The stones jutted out a little from the wall, and had markings on them, each stone with a number on it; one through nine.

The stones, except for the one at the top left that had the number '1', also had a few letters each.

So she needed to peck out some pattern. But what could it be?

She shifted her weight, painfully aware of the creature's steady breathing behind her.

Felicity almost looked, but stopped herself in time. She closed her eyes, focusing on her beating heart and wishing she could think more clearly.

How near was sunset?

Felicity opened her eyes and fluttered her wings, determined not to think about such things.

Her eyes moved over the rows of stones, wondering what the pattern was, and how she could guess it.

Her gaze stopped when she noticed something scratched into the stone wall nearly at its base.

The fat cap of the mushroom partly hid the words, but by tilting one way and then the other she could see the writing.

The scratched letters looked similar to what she had seen on the front door.

THE MORE you FEED ME, THE MORE I GROW. BUT IF you GIVE ME WATER, I WILL DIE IN ASHES. WHO AM I?

Felicity heaved a sigh. *Another* riddle.

Chapter 12

*F*elicity fluttered a little, keeping her balance on the stone lip of the little hollow in the wall. She needed to guess the riddle to open the queen's cell just like she'd had to guess the riddle on the front door to open it. But instead of speaking it, she needed to peck the stones that spelled out the answer.

How could she guess this riddle? Like the riddle on the front door, the answer was likely something very different from what she might first expect. But it would still make sense.

Should she hop back to the queen and ask her help in solving the riddle? Maybe, but that would take time and she would rather not hop back past Grak if she could figure out the riddle on her own.

Felicity sighed. What grew the more it ate? Pretty much everyone. Yet what died if it was *given* water? Everything alive needed water to live, so-

So it wasn't alive.

Felicity's heart leaped as her eyes fixed upon the word 'ASHES'.

That was a clue!

Ashes are made by *fire*!

Fire grew the more it was fed; but it died, a pile of damp ashes, if water fell on it!

Felicity nearly chirped in excitement that she had guessed the riddle so fast, but knowing who loomed behind her, she didn't dare make a noise.

She studied the stones above her. The letter 'F' was scratched beneath the number '3' on the stone in the upper right corner. The 'I' was on the stone on the left side of the middle row below the number '4'. The 'R' was on the bottom left corner below the '7'. And the last letter, 'E', was back on the '3' stone, just beside the 'F'.

"Three, four, seven, three," Felicity said beneath her breath. "Those are the stones I need to peck."

Pleased with herself, Felicity reached out to peck the '3'.

A crackle rattled her ears as a shock of pain raced through her from her beak down to her tail and Felicity jerked back. Her ears rang and her muscles jerked. A crackling sheet of something that looked like tiny bolts of lightning flickered in front of her beak.

She froze and shut her eyes, fearing the sound had wakened Grak. She did not dare look, but his breathing continued, unbroken. Relief crept through her aching body. He hadn't woken. But she hadn't even touched the stone either. Like something kept her out. Some kind of invisible fence.

Grak had been able to reach in to peck the stones, though. How come she couldn't?

Perhaps the sorcerer had made an enchantment that kept all others out but himself.

How could she save the queen now? Wake the Night Hawk and ask him to undo the lock? Of course not! Felicity shook her head. But how could she get past the invisible fence if only Grak could cross it?

Felicity's eyes narrowed but then widened at a hopeful thought. What if it only had to be a *part* of Grak? Like one of his feathers?

She couldn't pull one out of him. That would *hurt*, and he'd wake up! But what if-

Felicity's heart jumped. That feather!

That single molted feather longer than her whole body. It was still down there!

Just maybe-

She kept her focus from going to Grak as she spread her wings and dropped down from the lip of the alcove.

Hopping back around the huge bird, she found the long grey feather lying there just beneath the sharp spears of his curved toes.

Bending her head she took the quill in her beak, ignoring its pungent taste.

But then something happened.

Grak's breathing changed a little. A deep grumble echoed through the chamber. And in front of her face his toes uncurled.

Terrified, Felicity fell backward, sprawling on the stone floor, her wings outspread. In another moment his head would lift, and eyes, burning with fury, would look down at her over his terrible curved beak.

But nothing happened.

Grak only shifted his weight, grumbled, and went on sleeping.

Felicity rolled to her feet. She shook herself and turned back to pick up the feather again-

Only to see it curled beneath two of Grak's toes.

Oh dear.

She looked over her shoulder.

Across the distance, she could see the fairy queen watching.

The queen's hands clutched the bars of her cage as she peered through, her face white and tense.

Colin's face would be just as worried as he waited back home for Felicity to return with his mother. And so would his dad's.

Felicity couldn't let any of them down.

Drawing in a deep breath, she pulled all her courage in. She took a timid hop forward. Then another. And then she stood right at Grak's feet.

She bowed her head and took the quill in her beak. She pulled it a little, allowing herself a breath of relief as the plume began to slide through his toes.

Felicity's heart thumped as the feather whispered through Grak's talons. Could he feel the stiff plumes tickling his feet?

She had to be so careful!

Felicity slid her right foot a little way. Holding her breath, she did the same with her left. Grak continued to sleep. Allowing herself a tentative smile past the quill in her mouth, Felicity continued sliding along the floor, pulling the feather with her. It continued to come further, further. The plume rustled a little as it brushed through his toes-

And then-

It was free.

It fluttered, a bit crumpled, to the floor.

Relief washed through her in a wave.

But Felicity didn't have time to catch her breath. She was still in Grak's shadow and sunset couldn't be very far away.

Balancing Grak's molted feather in her beak, she hopped around him and fluttered up again to the little stone that jutted from the lip of the alcove.

Past the bitter-tasting feather in her mouth, Felicity drew a deep breath. Either this would work or- She didn't want to think about it not working.

Cautiously she poked the quill forward, her eyes half shut in anticipation of the crackle of light and the painful sting that came with it. But nothing happened. The quill continued forward through the invisible wall that would have kept her out, touched the back wall of the alcove, and scraped over the stone.

She drew in a deep breath, drew back a little, and poked the quill at the upper right stone with the '3'. It touched the stone. And the stone pushed in!

She drew back, and the stone rose back up again. Felicity drew in another breath before she moved the quill to the '4' and poked at it. The quill scraped a little and Felicity's heart jumped in her throat when it almost touched the '5' by mistake. What would happen if she pushed the wrong stone by accident?

Felicity's throat went dry. She didn't want to find out.

Drawing back, she poked the quill at the '4' again. It touched and the stone sank down, just like the first one.

She drew in a breath, struggling not to gag on the yucky taste of Grak's feather. Pulling back a little, she let the point of the quill drop until it touched the middle of the stone with the '7' on it. She pushed and the stone went in.

"*Ome more*," she whispered past the feather as she drew back. Her beak hurt from the strain of being so careful, and her muscles ached. But she lifted the quill toward the upper right corner again. It wavered a little but Felicity tightened her grip. She ignored the pain in her muscles, touched the quill to the center of the '3' and pushed the stone in.

Behind her a small pop echoed in the cavern, followed by a metallic clank.

She spun around to see the fairy queen push the door of her cage open and stumble out. The feather fell from Felicity's beak, and fluttered down to the floor beside Grak.

Dropping down to the floor, Felicity hopped past the sleeping Night Hawk as the fairy queen scrambled out into the weak light.

Felicity resisted the urge to chirp in delight as she flutter-hopped across the room.

She reached the queen who threw her arms around Felicity's neck. Then gripping both of Felicity's wings, the queen stepped back. She wore the crystal necklace around her neck now.

"Thank you dear, brave Felicity Sparrow," the queen said, her smile weary but grateful.

There was something wrong with the fairy, but Felicity's emotions were too great a mixture of joy and haste to think about what it could be.

How near was sunset?

Felicity bobbed her head. "You're sure welcome, ma'am. But let's get out of here."

The queen bit her lip, a doubtful look crossing her face. But she nodded and caught up the hem of her dirty dress as Felicity started to hop toward the darkened tunnel that would lead them out.

"But what will we do once we're out in the open air?" the queen asked, hurrying behind Felicity.

"Well, um," Felicity turned to look at the queen. Wasn't it obvious? "We'll fly back."

"Yes," Queen Lilia agreed, pursing her lips together. "But-"

Felicity stopped at the threshold into the tunnel as the realization hit her like a rock.

"You're wings are gone!" she choked.

"Grak clipped them off."

Felicity's eyes widened. "But- I thought fairy wings grew back if they get cut off!"

"They do, but every time they started growing, he clipped them. He wanted to make absolutely sure I couldn't escape."

"Ooh," Felicity seethed. "That- *stinker*!"

She glared back at the sleeping Night Hawk.

The feather she had used lay rumpled on the stone floor, and in a slightly different place than before. But other than that, Grak didn't look any different than when Felicity had first hopped into the chamber-

Until he stirred.

Chapter 13

*G*rak's head rose from behind him like the snake that had appeared from the grass by the fence.

The blood froze in her veins as everything Felicity imagined Grak to look like, came into view. His hooked beak that glimmered in the light of the mushrooms, his cold eyes-

There seemed to be something wrong with the color of his eyes, but in the dim light, Felicity couldn't guess what it could be.

Grak looked down at the feather at his feet. He blinked sleepily as he reached for it with a talon, and picked it up. He hadn't noticed the sparrow and fairy yet.

"*This isn't in the same place*," he said in a rough, deep voice that sounded like he had gravel in his throat.

"Run," Queen Lilia ordered in a harsh whisper, jerking Felicity out of her terrified stupor.

The queen gathered her skirts in one hand, grabbed Felicity's wing with the other, then turned and ran into the darkness of the tunnel, pulling the little sparrow along behind her.

The shadows of the corridor swallowed them.

Felicity's heart felt like it had climbed into her throat as she flutter-hopped with all her might beside the running fairy.

When would Grak noticed the queen missing?

Behind them, Grak's voice echoed through the tunnel, "*Something's different!*"

They rounded the first turn when the hawk's voice, angry now, rolled over them.

"*Someone's been here! Fairy! Who came in my-*"

A deafening silence cut off his words, shredded a moment later by a hawk's furious shriek.

"*What's this? Nooo!*"

A chirp of fright escaped Felicity. He'd discovered the empty cage!

"*Where is she? Where- is- my- fairy?*"

Crashing and clanking metal echoed down the tunnel. He must have flung the cage clear across the room!

Oh boy, he sounded mad!

"*She's gone!*" Grak screeched, his voice shrill with fury. "*My fairy's gone!*"

"What are we going to do?" the queen gasped, breathless as she ran.

"We'll be okay," Felicity chirped as they rushed around the next bend. "Once we're out I'll carry you on my back. And I know the password already. I figured out the riddle on the front of the door."

The stone that barred their escape came into view, illuminated by the little remaining sunlight that leaked in through the door.

"Rock!" Felicity sang out. "You're a rock!"

Nothing happened.

Gasping, the fairy and sparrow pulled to a halt.

"Rock, rock, rock!" Felicity cried.

The door did not move.

Behind them, an angry screech echoed through the tunnel.

"*Fairy!*" Grak shouted. "*Fairy, where are you?*"

Felicity and Queen Lilia exchanged a terrified glance before lifting their eyes to the door.

Writing scarred this side of the door, too. And it wasn't the same riddle as on the front.

Queen Lilia breathlessly read the scratched markings on the stone aloud:

I'M THE PART OF THE BIRD THAT'S NOT IN THE SKY.

I SPREAD OUT MY WINGS, YET I CANNOT FLY.

I CAN GO UNDERWATER, AND YET REMAIN DRY.

I FLEE WHEN YOU FOLLOW. TELL ME. WHO AM I?

Felicity's heart sank.

"*You're* a bird, Felicity! What part of you isn't in the sky?" the queen pleaded.

"*I'm coming to get you, fairy!*" Grak's furious voice shouted. "*You can't escape!*"

The sound of Grak's screeches and threats echoed toward them along the corridor.

Felicity looked back in the direction they'd come. What part of a bird *wasn't* in the sky?

"A nest?" she cried, desperate.

Nothing happened.

The queen looked back over her shoulder, struggling to speak in calm tones. "What isn't in the sky, spreads its wings, can be underwater and not get wet. And it flees if you follow it."

"I don't know!" Felicity beat her wings in fright. Her mind flashed over all the books she'd read.

"A *penguin*?" she wailed.

The door did not respond.

"Try to think like Grak," the queen pleaded. "After all, he wrote the riddles."

"I *can't* think like Grak!" Felicity insisted. "He's-"

Felicity cut herself off.

Did she *just maybe* know a little bit about how Grak might think? Just maybe?

She lifted her eyes to the riddle.

Even if Grak came out only at night, he would still see many of the same things she did.

Her mind tumbled over all she'd seen as she'd flown through Grak's domain.

The trees- The moths- The snake- But no.

All of those *would* get wet if they went in water. And while the moths had wings, they *did* fly. As for the snake, it didn't have wings at all. So that didn't work.

What about things that weren't alive?

The fence- The old overgrown road for the featherless two-foots' carts. The beetle- The little stream-

Felicity's mind screeched to a stop.

Something about the stream she'd flown over, connected to the riddle.

"*I can go underwater, and yet remain dry,*" she muttered.

Her eyes went wide as she snatched upon a thought, and she opened her beak-

"*There you are!*"

Felicity's thoughts flew apart as she and the queen spun around. The hawk, dirty grey and towering above them, stalked round the corner and stopped in the middle of the corridor. He glared at them with eyes that glowed red.

Felicity stiffened with fear. *Red eyes*!

A wicked smile curled up the corners of his hooked beak.

"And you have a little friend!" he guffawed, his voice making the rock beneath her feet shiver. *"I thought you might! You didn't get out of the guest room all on your own!"*

Felicity looked up at Grak as the sorcerer hawk stomped nearer, petrifying her with his red eyes.

She was supposed to do something. *What*?

She had been thinking about the stream she'd flown over, her own silhouette with wings outspread, darting over the trees and grass, dipping under the water of the stream, rippling across the rocks at the bottom and back out again on the other side, *without getting wet*!

The hawk strode nearer, his red eyes fixed on her with a look of cruel (and hungry) satisfaction.

"*What do you have to say for yourself,* sparrow?"

"Um," she stammered, "*shadow?*"

The hawk came to a dead stop, and the look of triumph on his face melted into angry dismay. "*How-?*" Grak demanded.

A moment later, the stone door began to scrape across the floor. A slice of dying sunlight spilled into the tunnel and began to widen.

Grak shook his head as if bringing himself out of a stupor. "*How did you guess-?*" he roared as he scampered forward.

"Let's go!" Felicity cried. She snatched the queen's sleeve in her beak and they darted out through the slowly opening doorway. The sky beyond the end of the tunnel glowed crimson.

"Get on my back!" Felicity shouted. "And hold on tight!"

Queen Lilia scrambled on the sparrow's back as a screech of rage followed them.

The scrape and scree of talons scrabbling against stone assaulted Felicity's ears, and shivered through her blood.

The door behind them was not fully open yet, and Grak, his bulk still unable to fit through, pushed against it, trying to force it to move faster. His talons gouged furious scars into the stone floor beneath him.

Felicity turned forward again, focusing on the end of the tunnel. Spreading her wings, she hopped several steps, leapt into the air, and shot out into the sky.

Beating her wings, she dashed southward. To her right, the sun sat on a long bank of clouds like a lazy red frog on a wide lily pad.

"*Foolish little bird!*" Grak screeched, his voice echoing off the face of the tall cliff. "*Do you think a mere sparrow can outfly me?*"

An angry scream followed as Grak dove off the ledge.

"He's coming," Queen Lilia cried.

"I see him!" Felicity gasped.

She banked hard to the left and felt a whoosh of air as Grak zoomed past.

The hawk turned in the air in front of her and wheeled back, his claws stretching out.

"Hold on!" Felicity cried. Queen Lilia grabbed handfuls of feathers just before Felicity dropped sharply. Once again, Grak barely missed them.

"We won't be able to dodge him forever!" the queen cried.

"We've got to try!" Felicity insisted, breathless. "And- I have an idea!"

She beat her wings fiercely as the tree tops dropped away and the clearing where she'd met the snake opened beneath her.

There, running down the middle of the open grassy space, she saw the chain link fence.

"Now, this is important, ma'am!" she cried into the wind as she sped across the wide clearing. "You need to duck down as much as you can! Hold on tight! And no matter what, *keep your head down*!"

The queen obeyed.

Felicity couldn't see him, so Grak was probably straight behind her, right in the one spot where she couldn't see. But she imagined his cruel, curving claws stretching out to snatch both her and the queen out of the air.

Felicity swerved to the side and dropped heavily before catching herself again.

A scream of frustration tore through the air behind them.

She beat her wings, skimming over the tops of the grass.

Queen Lilia's fists held tightly to her feathers, the fairy folded down against her back.

"You think you can escape, sparrow?" Grak screeched. *"You think you can dodge me forever?"*

Felicity did not let herself falter or look back as she sped forward, flapping with all her strength, her eyes fixed unmoving on her target straight ahead.

The chain link fence flew to meet her with astonishing speed. If she timed this just right-

At the very last moment, Felicity tucked her wings tight against her body—

The wind screamed in her ears as she and the fairy queen blasted through the center of the diamond-shaped link, followed a second later by a jangling crash and a squawk of surprised wrath.

Felicity spread her wings and shot up into the air then circled, looking back.

Grak lay sprawled on his back, his wings outspread. The chain link fence still vibrated from the high speed collision.

Beside him, something long and black writhed on the ground.

"You clumsssy sssorcccerer! You sssquished me!" complained the snake that had tried to eat Felicity earlier in the day.

"*Oh, shut up, you idiotic serpent!*" Grak groaned.

"Idiotic, you sssay? I'm not the sssimpleton who crassshed into the fenccce!"

The hawk shook his head to clear it, and his red eyes glared upward, fixing on Felicity and the queen. "*You!*"

Felicity whirled away, beating her wings southward.

"*You!*" he squawked after them, his voice fading. "*You- sparrooooow!*"

But neither Felicity nor Queen Lilia looked back.

Chapter 14

*F*elicity allowed herself to slow down a little as she soared over the tops of the trees. Even though the fairy queen weighed less than Colin had, the race away from Grak had been exhausting. Her muscles ached but she didn't dare land to rest until they crossed the border.

But what would happen then? Would the trees try to keep Queen Lilia in like they kept the other fairies out? Felicity hoped not.

The last sliver of the sun sank below the horizon, glimmered one last time, and then disappeared. Just then, Felicity heard a familiar sound.

Woosha!

She looked toward the sound to see angry eyes set above a frowning mouth fluttering up out of the trees.

"Ha ha!" she laughed, unafraid. "It's one of those moths!"

The queen turned to look. "Oh, dear," she said. "Thank the goodnesses there's only one."

"Oh, it's not dangerous," Felicity replied. "I know it looks like a monster face but it's just the wings of a moth."

"Yes, a ghost-face moth," the queen agreed. "That's what we fairies call them. They're Grak's servants, and they do whatever he tells them. They can't leave his realm. That's the only good thing about them."

Queen Lilia glanced over her shoulder. "When the sun is up or if there is only one, they're not so dangerous. But once the sun sets, if there are many of them-"

She trailed off.

"Oooh- What happens if there are lots?" Felicity asked.

"Well," the queen said. "We only saw the one, so-"

Shawoosha woosha!

Several more moths flew up out of the canopy.

Felicity's heart climbed up into her throat. The moths were following them.

"What happens, ma'am?" she chirped, picking up speed.

To her dismay, the moths sped up as well.

"They'll latch onto us!" Queen Lilia leaned lower as wind began to whip past them. "They're small, but many together can lift both of us and carry us back to Grak."

"Oooh, dear!" Felicity didn't like the idea of a hundred moths latching onto her with their icky, pricky feet, let alone being carried back to the sorcerer hawk, especially after she had made him crash into that fence. Now he'd be *really* mad!

"But I think they can't follow us as easily down in the forest itself," the fairy queen said. "Try to find an opening in the trees!"

"But I'll lose my way when I'm down there!"

Shawoosha, woosha! Woosha woosha!

Behind them *dozens* of moths filled the darkening air. A wall of flapping wings followed them.

And the moths were gaining!

"I'll guide you," the fairy queen promised.

"Ooo- okay-" The next dark opening Felicity saw in the canopy, she dove down into the dark.

Shadows closed around her, and for a moment she couldn't see at all. The forest had been dim during the day, but now it was nearly pitch black!

"Watch out for that tree!" the queen cried. Felicity dipped to the right, avoiding the gnarled silhouette of a tree that loomed out of the darkness in front of her.

"Bear toward the right!" The queen pointed forward and to the right. Felicity obeyed.

The forest was a tangle of shadows against darker shadows. Felicity could not have found her way without the queen's guidance.

Shawoosha, woosha! Woosha, woosha, woosha!

Behind her, several of the moths followed but not as many as she'd seen above the canopy. They careened from side to side like they were confused, or blind. But they *were* still coming.

"Left, around this tree! Now straight on, ahead!"

Felicity obeyed the queen's order.

Shawoosha, woosha! *Woosha, woosha!*

Behind them, the pack of moths drew steadily closer.

"Ooooh, deeear!" Felicity wailed. This was just like her nightmare! It was coming true!

"Don't panic!" the queen cried. "Look up there!"

Ahead of them, amongst the shadows against darker shadows, pricks of white light began to wink on. A little group of stars in the darkness. Except they were down inside the forest! Fairy lanterns!

"They're waiting for us!" Lilia cheered.

Felicity felt a leap of joy swell up in her heart but in the next moment a cry of fright escaped the queen.

Wood creaked and leaves rustled like sinister, wordless whispering as a shadow swooped down.

Felicity chirped in fright and ducked to the side. The branch barely missed snatching the fairy off of her back. Its forked twigs, shaped like a bony hand, closed in an empty fist and faded away behind them.

But it wasn't the last! From left and right, the enchanted trees at the edge of Grak's domain were beginning to stir. Skinny wooden twigs, shaped like grasping fingers snatched at the queen. Felicity found herself rising and falling, swerving left and right to stay ahead of the skeletal branches as well as the moths that were gaining ground behind them.

The lights of the fairy lanterns drew closer but with all the dodging and ducking, fear swelled in her that they wouldn't make it before a branch grabbed the queen or the moths reached them and plucked her off.

Shawoosha!

The moth at the front of the swarm veered closer, reaching in to grab at the queen with its prickly feet.

But as the moth reached out for her, the queen balled a fist. "Take that!" Lilia cried and swung, punching the moth right in its puffy mouth.

The moth reeled back. But it recovered quickly, and flapped near again.

Its face remained expressionless, but furious sparks glimmered in its multi-faceted eyes.

"No! No, no!" Felicity chirped, dipping and swerving to escape the angry creature. These moths couldn't be shaken! But she *would not* let them take the queen!

Just as its prickly foreleg reached out for the queen again, something whistled out of the middle of the cluster of little white lamps and smacked the moth right between its bulging eyes.

The moth tumbled away, head over wings from the force of the blow. Felicity caught a glimpse of a green mess splattered across its face before it floundered away and was lost in darkness.

Other moths were still coming. But now the air filled with a whirr as little green peas came flying out of the cluster of little lights. They splattered into moths and into the grasping fingers of branches with damp squishing sounds.

The skinny branches flinched and withdrew and the moths fell back amidst the onslaught of peas as Felicity and the queen shot out of the reach of the grasping branches and into a cluster of hovering fairies. Some held little white lanterns shaped like flower buds in their hands; many others clutched rose thorn spears. Several, including Colin and his father, held sling shots loaded with fat peas. King Taron's arm looked good as new, and Colin's wings had regrown, gleaming in the lamp light. Golly, fairies healed fast!

"Taron!" Lilia cried. "Colin!"

"Lilia!" the king shouted as Colin cried, "Mother!"

Colin turned and flapped toward Felicity as Taron drew back the stretchy band of his slingshot and fired one last pea into the group of moths that reeled and recoiled, retreating into the darkness.

Felicity alighted in the crook of a tree behind the fairies

The queen slid from her back and rushed down the branch into the arms of Colin and her husband amidst the cheers of the other fairies.

Felicity shifted her weight so that she could hop down the branch to see Colin. But changing her mind, she settled back, surprised that she felt so tired all of a sudden.

Then again, she'd been flying for her life for the last several hours and now that the danger was finally gone-

She'd stay here for a minute, she told herself. Just a minute. Then she'd get up.

She folded her wings across her back and settled down in the comfortable little crook that cradled her like a nest. Her eyelids felt heavy. A huge yawn escaped her beak.

"Felicity!" Colin cried.

Her eyelids fluttered open briefly as the young fairy darted up the branch. "Hey Colin," she muttered flatly.

"You did it! You brought my mother back!" He threw his arms around her neck.

"Um-" Her mind had a hard time thinking. Her thoughts felt so fuzzy and comfortable. Her eyelids drooped again. "Oh. Yeah. It was- it was great. Grak was- Grak was a great big- a big- big-"

Felicity didn't finish her sentence. Her eyes fell shut instead, and she began to snore.

Chapter 15

*M*usic echoed through the palace as Felicity hopped at Colin's side along a brightly lit corridor.

She didn't remember being carried back to the palace or to the nest of cattail down where she'd woken up after a lovely sleep. But she was here now.

Everything seemed brighter than before. And everyone she passed had something nice to say to her!

Little lamps hung on the walls or from the ceiling, swaying gently in the air, their light dancing off the white walls and floors.

The music came from somewhere up ahead.

The sound, singing and flutes mixed with the merry patter of drums, grew louder and louder as the pair neared the throne room.

But when the archway passed over their heads and the big room came into view, everyone turned to look at her, and fell silent. But it was only for just a moment before everybody started clapping.

King Taron and Queen Lilia stood up from their thrones at the front of the room. Colin hurried forward to stand beside his mother whose lovely rainbow-colored wings were already starting to grow back again.

Felicity though, hung back in the doorway, feeling uncertain and shy.

"Felicity Augustina Sparrow."

Around the room, the applause faded at the king's voice. Every face was fixed on her.

"Yes?" Her timid voice echoed in the room.

The king smiled. "Come forward, please."

The little sparrow gulped and hopped forward. Standing beside his mother, Colin offered Felicity a small wave as she came near and stopped at the base of the steps. She offered her friend a hasty grin.

The king spoke again. "Because of you Mistress Sparrow, our queen is returned to us."

Taron lifted his hand, which held the queen's, for everybody to see. Cheers and applause again filled the room.

"We can never repay what you did for her and for our folk." The king's smile grew warm. "And for our family."

The king and queen traded a smile before Lilia turned to the room and spoke. "Felicity Sparrow braved the lair of Grak the wicked sorcerer to save me at great peril to herself. She solved three difficult riddles that stood between us and freedom. She outsmarted the Night Hawk himself and outflew his minions."

More clapping filled the room.

Felicity ducked her head at the praise.

"Thank you Felicity," the queen said, more softly now. "I owe you my life."

Felicity looked up to see both the queen and king with tears shining in their eyes.

"And we all owe you our thanks," Taron added.

Colin asked, "Is there anything we can do to for you, Felicity?"

Felicity tipped her head to the side. "Well, um, hmm."

She didn't *need* anything she didn't already have. So long as her home was still there when she got back.

And especially her beloved books.

Some beetles would be nice. But it might be a bad idea to ask for them. Fairies didn't seem to like eating bugs and she could find those on her own anyway.

Then she caught on an idea.

"Well, um, maybe you could keep an eye out for Augustus? I don't know if he's even still, well, you know, around. But-"

Felicity's voice trailed away.

Lilia smiled and the king bowed in agreement.

"Of course," Taron said. "And if *you* see him, tell him to come visit us when he is able. He was a good friend to our folk."

"Is there anything else we can do?" Lilia asked.

"Well," Felicity shrugged. "Not really. I guess I just- I'm ready to go home."

The queen's eyes softened. With a smile Lilia said, "If you want nothing else from us, dear Felicity, I hope you'll take this."

Felicity's eyes opened in surprise as the queen reached up and drew the crystal necklace over her head.

"This is yours now," the queen said. She held out the necklace, the glittering crystal resting in her palm. "For you are one of us. If you want to be."

The little sparrow's beak opened. "Oh my gosh! Yeah!"

Lilia smiled, and Felicity bowed as the fairy queen descended the steps.

A moment later, the necklace slipped over her head and around Felicity's neck.

"Take this as a symbol of our friendship," the queen said. "You will always be a friend of the fairy folk, welcome here and in the Wildwood where our power extends."

The little sparrow looked up, warmed by the queen's smile. Lilia touched a hand gently to Felicity's head before returning up the steps to take the king's hand again.

As Felicity straightened and turned to face the crowd of fairies, applause filled the chamber, mingled with voices cheering her name.

Felicity bobbed her head and grinned, her new necklace glimmering in the light of the many lamps.

Chapter 16

*T*he flight back home through the forest was pretty uneventful. A nice change after the last few perilous days. Colin had offered to fly her home, since Felicity was still unfamiliar with the Wildwood, and she was grateful for his company.

Now that his wings were grown back to full size, Colin didn't need to ride, and flew beside her instead.

They had no need to hurry, and Felicity liked seeing different sights along the way that she'd missed before.

Colin showed her the oldest tree in the Wildwood, a short, fat, gnarled thing that grew in a rare patch of sunlight, surrounded by taller trees. Felicity could have guessed it was pretty old, even without Colin telling her. Still, it bore leaves, and families of squirrels, and while Felicity couldn't tell trees' emotions, it seemed to be happy enough.

He also showed her a ring of mushrooms in a small clearing where they had fairy parties now and then.

Being an honorary fairy herself, she was welcome to come when they had festivals.

Their next one would be the summer solstice, Colin said. They'd have games and music, and all sorts of food.

With a playful grin, Colin promised that he might even be able to find a couple of beetles, just for her.

Felicity brightened at that.

Being an honorary fairy sure had its perks!

Felicity and Colin emerged from the Wildwood to a deep orange sunset fading in the west, and fireflies winking in the twilight. With her friend beside her, she fluttered to a branch and looked over the wide black road the featherless- the *persons* had made. (If the fairies had made her an honorary fairy it wouldn't hurt to think like one.)

A whir of air increased in sound and a pair of giant bright eyes came around a bend. A person's cart drew near, rumbled by, and then continued down the road, leaving them in quiet darkness.

And there, on the other side of the road, waited her own tree! The welcoming lights of fireflies twinkled among the branches.

It had only been two days, but it seemed like it had been seasons since she left home with Colin on her back.

The road was quiet as they flew across it. Still, Felicity cast a nervous glance upward. It was too dark for hawks, but owls might be out.

"I wouldn't worry about that." Colin said, guessing her thoughts. He chuckled and added, "Word has gotten around that you practically beat the feathers off of Grak. I don't think you- or *we*- will get much trouble from any large birds from now on."

They made their way into the tangle of leaves, past the twigs where Colin's poor shins had banged pretty hard, and landed on the branch outside of Felicity's door.

"Well, I'll see you later." Colin reached out a hand like he had when they'd first introduced themselves. "Promise you'll come to the summer solstice in the fairy ring?"

"You bet," Felicity returned. She held out her wing. He grasped the end of it, giving it a good shake.

"I'll see you there!" He lifted off the branch.

Felicity hopped a little after him and watched as Colin wove his way out of the tree and flew across the road.

Once he reached the edge of the Wildwood, he perched on the branch of a tree and turned back, lifting his hand once more. She waved a wing.

Then Colin rose off the branch and darted away into the shadows.

Sighing, Felicity turned and hopped into her home. She paused in the doorway and looked around.

With the fireflies outside, plenty of light filled the room, illuminating her books, her nest, the icebox. Everything looked just as it had before-

Wait just a minute!-

On the bottom of the framed picture of the two ivory-billed woodpeckers, a small white flower rested. It lay there so carefully it couldn't have just blown in through the door.

And there- on the edge of her nest, sat a scrap of paper. With- *writing* on it!

Hopping to it, she read the words:

My Dear Felicity,

Congratulations on your successful adventure! I am pleased that you rescued Queen Lilia, and put Grak in his place as well! Perhaps he will learn better manners from his encounter with you. Or not. In any case, I thought you might enjoy some fresh beetles. I have left them in the icebox.

"Ohh!" Felicity chirped and hopped to the icebox, opening the door. As promised, five fat beetles, still wiggling, lay on a little leaf on the middle shelf.

"Yummy!"

She plucked out the fattest one in her beak and turned back to the letter, munching the bug down as she read.

> I couldn't be prouder of you, my dear, even if you were my own chick. You are a brave, magnificent little sparrow. Truly one in a quadrillilion. And I hope you always remember that.
>
> All my best,
>
> A. I. W.

"A. I. W.?" she asked herself.

Had Augustus been here while she was gone? This looked like his writing. And she didn't know anyone else with the initials *A. I. W.* Especially not someone who could write or who would be so generous as to leave *five* fat beetles in her icebox!

She'd have to show the letter to Colin and his folks the next time she saw them.

But for now-

Felicity turned toward her bookshelf, remembering the story she'd been reading when she first met Colin. She hadn't finished it yet!

She fluttered to the shelf, found the book, and pulled it from between the others.

With a contented breath, she hopped into her nest and opened her book to the page where she'd left off.

Snuggling down, Felicity began to read.

In Loving Memory-

Alvin E. Salima

1964-2014

One of the greatest souls I have ever had the privilege of

meeting.

Valerie Anne Pohaiamepumehanaakealoha Akau Meli

1969-2014

Felicity was fortunate to have such a great teacher as

Augustus. And I was fortunate to have such a great senpai

as you. Thanks for all that you taught me.

神よ, また 会う まで

About the Author

Some of Loralee Evans' earliest memories are of sitting with her mom or dad while they read her stories like *The Tale of Peter Rabbit* by Beatrix Potter, or *Make Way for Ducklings* by Robert McCloskey. These memories, along with many great teachers who got her excited about reading, are what helped her develop a love of books, and of writing. She has lived in Missouri, Texas, and Utah, and even spent a year and a half in Japan. Some of her favorite authors are James Dashner, Harper Lee, C.S. Lewis, Heather B. Moore, Rachel Ann Nunes, Candace Salima, J. Scott Savage, J.R.R. Tolkien, and Julie Wright.

Felicity~ A Sparrow's Tale is her fourth book.

Read more about her books on her website,
www.loraleeevans.com

Or visit her blog,
loraleeevansauthor.blogspot.com

You can also follow her on Twitter: **@EvansLoralee**

51598456R00112

Made in the USA
Charleston, SC
28 January 2016